$\mathcal{A}$ CANDLELIGHT ROMANCE

Candlelight Romances

CAPTURED BY LOVE

Jean Hager

A CANDLELIGHT ROMANCE

Published by
Dell Publishing Co., Inc.
1 Dag Hammarskjold Plaza
New York, New York 10017

Dell ® TM 681510, Dell Publishing Co., Inc.

ISBN: 0-440-11122-6

Printed in the United States of America
First printing—May 1981

FOR ELAINE

CAPTURED BY LOVE

ONE

Leigh Alexander stood outside Professor Harlan's office and looked through the hall window at the campus green below. It was a brilliant Oklahoma spring morning and the clumps of iris, forsythia, and Japanese quince bordering the narrow walkways that intersected the oval green were a riot of purple, yellow, and red. Leigh leaned forward, resting her elbows on the windowsill, and let the soft breeze play with her long, fair hair. The loose, natural waves that swept away from a center part and framed her oval face fell forward as she gazed down at the students strolling across the green. Leigh brushed the long strands back with both hands, exposing dark arched brows and long, sooty lashes that framed violet-blue eyes—eyes which, at the moment, were blurred by a film of moisture. The familiar scene below had created in her a wave of bittersweet nostalgia. This campus, which had been home for six years, must be left behind now as Leigh, armed with a brand-new diploma in veterinary medicine, went out to face the real world.

As she straightened, dashing the mist from her eyes with the back of her hand, a tall red-haired young man came out of Professor Harlan's office.

"Leigh! Hi." A pleased smile lighted Bruce Landing's ruddy face.

"Hello, Bruce," Leigh said, smiling in return. Bruce always made her feel more cheerful. He was an incurable optimist. "You look as if you've had some good news."

Bruce's grin widened even more. "The best! Remember that big vet clinic in San Antonio I told you about? Pro-

11

fessor Harlan just told me they've offered me a job. I start work Monday."

"Oh, Bruce, that's wonderful!" Leigh exclaimed and threw her arms around the young man's neck, giving him a fierce hug. "I knew you'd get it. After all, you were class valedictorian."

He looked down at her, his head cocked to one side, a teasing gleam in his green eyes. "Hey, why don't I go back into the office, come out and tell you again—so you can give me another hug? Maybe you could even throw in a little kiss this time."

She laughed. "Forget it, buster. Only one hug per customer today."

"Aw, gee," he drawled good-naturedly. "Hey, what about you? Did you accept that offer from the vet in Oklahoma City?"

"Not yet." She chewed her bottom lip thoughtfully. "You know a small animal clinic was never my first choice."

"You mean you don't relish catering to society matrons and their perfumed poodles?"

"I have nothing against poodles," Leigh said, "or society matrons either. But I specialized in the care of horses, remember?"

"Ah, yes." Bruce shook his head in mock indulgence. "And all your friends tried to tell you it was a mistake."

"All you male chauvinists, you mean!" Leigh shot back. "Only big, strong men can handle horses. Right?"

Bruce patted her head with a big hand, as if he were calming an impetuous child. "Come on, Leigh. That's not fair. I know you can handle the mighty beasts as well as any man in our class. In fact, I never saw anyone who understood horses the way you do. You can practically make them talk to you. But your customers won't know that, and they're going to have trouble believing it when they see you—all hundred pounds of you."

"One hundred and eight," she said, correcting him. "I gained weight this year."

Bruce studied her doubtfully. "That must be with your winter coat and boots on."

12

She wrinkled her nose at him. "I have to go in to see the professor. I really am happy about your job, Bruce."

Hurriedly he took a crumpled piece of paper from his pocket. "Here's the name and address of the clinic where I'll be working. Write me when you get settled."

She took the paper and tucked it into her skirt pocket. "I will."

His green eyes regarded her with a sudden solemnity. "Promise?"

"Yes."

"I can always run you down through the professor," he warned.

"That won't be necessary," she said, laughing. "I'll let you know where I am." It would be comforting to keep in touch with Bruce after she had moved to a strange place and started a new job. Although she knew that Bruce would like their relationship to be more than friendly, she had never been able to see him in a romantic light; but he was a very good friend, and she valued that friendship.

He touched her cheek lightly. "Good luck, Doctor Alexander."

"Same to you, Doctor Landing."

He went off down the hall, whistling.

Leigh entered Professor Harlan's office. The elderly, gray-haired man behind the big oak desk was on the telephone. He looked up and greeted her with a smile, motioning for her to take a chair.

"I understand, Mr. Casey," he was saying. "I have the very person you're looking for. Doctor Leigh Alexander specialized in the care of horses and was in the top ten percent of the graduating class. You couldn't go wrong there. Of course, Doctor Alexander has had several offers so you would have to make a hasty decision on this." He winked broadly at Leigh. Upon hearing the professor's remark about horses, Leigh's heartbeat had quickened. She sat down in one of the wooden chairs across the desk from him and twisted her fingers nervously in her lap.

"What's that?" the professor was saying. "Next Wednesday?" He raised questioning eyebrows at Leigh and she nodded vigorously. "I'm certain Doctor Alexander can be

13

there by then. Why don't we leave it this way. If the doctor is delayed, I'll call you back. Fine, that sounds like a fair arrangement. You're quite welcome. Good-bye, Mr. Casey." He replaced the receiver and looked at Leigh, a satisfied smile spreading across his face.

"It's a job offer, isn't it? Who was that on the phone, Uncle Jess?" It was a courtesy title, for he was no relation, merely a longtime family friend who had become Leigh's guardian when her parents were killed in an automobile accident six years earlier. In fact, it was largely Jess Harlan's influence that had prompted Leigh to go into veterinary medicine. He had pointed out that she could combine her lifelong love of horses with a satisfying career, and he had convinced her that the field was opening up to females as never before. The barriers of prejudice against women were toppling on every hand, according to Uncle Jess. Leigh, however, had discovered, as one of six girls in a class of eighty, that a few of those barriers still stood. She had been the brunt of several practical jokes perpetrated by male students during the past three years as a vet student—some of the jokes were merely good-natured teasing, but others were expressions of hidden resentment.

"That, my dear girl, was Shane Casey," Jess Harlan said in answer to her question, "owner of one of the largest quarter-horse ranches in the state of Texas."

"Oh, *that* Shane Casey!" Leigh had read articles about the man in the horse journals that came to the school. Shane Casey was known across the country for the high-quality quarter horses he bred on his Texas ranch. He was one of the wealthiest men in Texas; his picture was often seen on society pages of southwestern newspapers, usually with a beautiful woman or two hanging on his arm.

"Uncle Jess," Leigh said, leaning forward to peer into his warm brown eyes, which were partially hidden by the slightly tinted spectacles he wore. "Does Shane Casey know I'm a woman?"

Jess Harlan threw both hands out in an exaggerated gesture of innocence. "I didn't lie to the man, Leigh. You

14

heard what I said." He reached across the desk and took her hand in both of his. "You're a good vet, honey. Don't start doubting yourself now."

"You kept referring to me as Doctor Leigh Alexander. Leigh can also be spelled L-E-E when it's a man's name. You *didn't* tell him I'm a woman, did you?"

He gave her hand a final squeeze and got to his feet. "I couldn't see what that had to do with your abilities as a veterinarian," he grumbled. "Now how about having lunch with an old codger in the campus cafeteria?"

"Doctor Alexander has had several offers," Leigh mimicked her guardian pertly as they descended the stairs. "Why haven't I heard about all those offers?"

He grinned sheepishly. "The one in Oklahoma City was firm, and I'm sure there would have been others in time."

When they had filled their trays and found a table in the cafeteria, Leigh said, "Why don't you retire, Uncle Jess? You're always talking about it. You could come with me to Texas—provided I decide to go."

Jess Harlan gave her a surprised look. "That's all you need, an old man hanging around, cramping your style. I suppose you intend for me to take care of the house or apartment or whatever you end up in. An overeducated housekeeper, eh?"

"No," she protested. "To tell the truth . . . I could use your moral support if I decide to accept Shane Casey's offer."

"Nonsense!" He made a clucking noise with his tongue. "You're going to go out there and wow them! How many vets do you know who are beautiful as well as competent? You'll make history, honey."

"Stop teasing me, Uncle Jess," Leigh said, suddenly serious. "In some ways it would be easier if I were ugly as sin. Then . . . at least . . . people would judge me only on my ability. That's all I want, you know, merely a chance to prove what I can do." She gazed across the table at the elderly man, noticing with a pang the weary slump of his shoulders. "That and the opportunity to repay you a little for all you've done for me. That's why I want you to retire now. Let me take care of you for a change."

Jess Harlan laughed. "I don't need taking care of, my dear girl. Besides, you don't owe me anything. You know, ever since my wife died years ago, I've regretted having no children. You're the daughter I never had, Leigh. But I'm too set in my ways to change my life-style now. I expect I'll die teaching, if the university will keep me on that long."

"Don't talk about dying." Leigh had known Jess Harlan all her life, and during the last six years, living with him in his comfortable apartment near the campus, she had come to love him as a second father. He had been there to comfort and shelter her when it had seemed her shattered world could never be put back together again.

He cleared his throat and removed his glasses, polishing them slowly with a paper napkin. "Shane Casey wants a vet to live on his ranch and take care of his quarter horses." He replaced his glasses, settling them securely on his nose. "The salary he mentioned is better than most vets right out of school can make. He suggested that you come for a probationary period of three months. At the end of that time, if both parties are satisfied, he's willing to give you a longer contract, which would be renewed annually."

Having finished her salad and fruit, Leigh pushed her tray aside. "It sounds fine except for the tiny detail I mentioned before. When Shane Casey discovers I'm a woman, he will more than likely tell me to turn around and go back where I came from."

"He gave his word that you'd be given a three months trial," Jess Harlan said stoutly. "Shane Casey is not the sort of man to go back on his word."

"I know, Uncle Jess, but I don't like deceit."

Grumbling, he pushed a cold piece of meat loaf about on his plate with his fork. "No one is being deceived. If Shane Casey had asked your sex, I'd have told him." He paused, then looked at her sharply. "You have to go after what you want in this world, Leigh. And you've never been one to back down without a fight. Unless, of course"—one corner of his mouth twitched slightly—"you're afraid of Shane Casey."

16

"Afraid! What an absurd idea!"

"Good!" he said triumphantly. "It's settled then. You'll go to Texas. And while we're on that subject, I hope you'll let me give you some advice. How old are you now?"

She grinned. "You don't have a subtle bone in your body, do you? You know very well I'm twenty-four."

"Yes, and you've been too busy until now to think about marriage, although I did hope at one time that something might develop between you and young Landing." He brightened. "I just remembered, Landing's going to San Antonio. That's less than fifty miles from the Casey Ranch."

"Oh, really?" Leigh said lightly. "Well, you can get that calculating gleam out of your eye, Uncle Jess. I could never think of Bruce as anything but a friend."

"Oh." He looked deflated. "What about those other young men who take you out occasionally?"

She shook her head.

"None of them will do, eh? Oh, well, now that you're leaving our insular little university world, you'll be meeting other young men. You shouldn't be devoting all your time to a career. You're a warm and lovely girl. You need a husband and children to be completely fulfilled. I want to hold my grandchildren on my knee before I'm too senile to enjoy it."

"I have plenty of time," she said with an easy smile, "and so do you."

Leigh left early Tuesday morning for Texas. Her five-year-old red Volkswagen had been serviced only last week. It was the last day of May, bright and clear, and in spite of her doubts, Leigh felt a sense of exhilaration. She reached Dallas before dark and found a reasonably priced motel for the night. Early the next morning after a hearty breakfast she resumed her journey and reached San Antonio by early afternoon.

After some searching, she found the correct highway leading out of San Antonio. It led through a few small towns and eventually became a narrow two-lane, blacktop road.

The country through which she passed, part of the fertile Rio Grande Valley, was vibrantly alive with spring grasses; its shallow rolling hills appeared to be careless drapes and folds in a vast expanse of green velvet. She knew she could come to love this country if only Shane Casey did not, as she feared, prove to be intractably opposed to female veterinarians.

The last little town she passed through before reaching the ranch was called San Lorenzo, one more reminder of the Spanish heritage of this part of the state. Actually it was hardly a town at all, merely a scattering of modest frame-houses, a filling station, and a few stores. On the southern edge of San Lorenzo stood a large, modern brick school building. From its size Leigh surmised the school must serve students from several miles around.

A mile or so past the school she caught sight of a large sign that announced in big black letters that the Casey Ranch was four miles farther along. The bold sign brought home to Leigh with disquieting force the nearness of her destination and, at the thought of presenting herself there as the new veterinarian, she felt a queasy sensation in the pit of her stomach.

Her attention was suddenly distracted by a small barefoot boy who was trudging alongside the road. He carried worn canvas shoes across one shoulder, holding on to them by the laces. At the sound of her approaching car, the boy turned a tan face in her direction and flashed white teeth in a captivating smile. His free hand went up, thumb extended.

She braked her Volkswagen and, as soon as it had come to a stop, the child was clambering into the seat beside her. She saw now that he was Mexican and that he couldn't be older than eight or nine.

"You're awfully young to be out here alone," she greeted him as she pulled back onto the road. He was settling his canvas shoes in his lap and did not reply.

"Hitchhiking can be dangerous," she went on. "You must be in a terrific hurry to get somewhere. Are you in some kind of trouble?"

He turned large brown eyes on her and flashed another

smile. "No trouble, señorita. I hitchhike many times. Everyone around here knows me. My father works at the Casey Ranch." He added the last proudly. "My name is Manuel Gomez."

Leigh couldn't help returning his irrepressible grin. "Happy to meet you, Manuel. I'm Leigh Alexander. Shouldn't you be in school?"

"I am out of school for the day, señorita." Manuel's joyous expression told her school was not one of his favorite places.

"It's only two thirty now. Did they let out early today?"

"Early, yes." Manuel nodded happily.

His English was heavily accented, and Leigh suspected that Spanish was spoken in his home. "Isn't there a school bus? According to the sign I passed a while back, the school is five miles from the ranch."

Manuel nodded again. "Sometimes I like to walk." He wiggled the toes on the small, dirty feet that extended over the edge of the seat. "But today my feet were tired." He shrugged carelessly. "Anyway, someone always comes along to give me a ride. Like you, señorita." His grin was mischievous.

Leigh laughed. "I see. Well, this is your lucky day, Manuel. It happens that I am going to the Casey Ranch too."

Manuel regarded her quizzically. "Many pretty ladies come to the ranch, señorita."

I'll just bet they do, Leigh thought, remembering the pictures on the society pages.

"I have never seen you before," Manuel went on.

"I've never been to the ranch before, Manuel," Leigh told him. "I'm the new veterinarian."

Manuel stumbled over the word *veterinarian*, then gazed at her with incomprehension. "You will explain to me what this means?"

"I'm going to take care of the horses."

The child's liquid brown eyes grew wide. "You—you, señorita, are taking the place of Doctor Smith?" He pronounced it *Smeeth.*

19

"If Doctor Smith took care of the horses, yes, I am his replacement."

Manuel frowned. "None of the other pretty ladies have ever taken care of the horses. You are not—what do you say?—pulling my leg?"

Leigh laughed. "No. I really am the new veterinarian, Doctor Leigh Alexander." Inwardly she sighed, thinking that here male chauvinism seemed to take root at a young age.

All of a sudden Manuel started to laugh. "Oh, you are very funny," he sputtered after several moments. "A señorita horse doctor!"

"You're a big help!" Leigh said wryly. "I have a feeling your reaction is typical of what I can expect at the ranch."

Manuel choked back his laughter. "Señorita, don't worry. I will be, as you say, a big help." He squared his shoulders and arranged his mischievous face into a grave expression. "You will need a strong man to help you with the horses. I am much stronger than I look, señorita. You will not even need to get your beautiful hands dirty."

"That wasn't exactly what I had in mind," Leigh told him, amused. "I'm used to getting my hands dirty. It's part of my job."

"I will help you," he told her again.

Even a child has little faith in me, Leigh thought ruefully. "*Amigo*," she said, "you are not the only male on the Casey Ranch who is in for a surprise."

At her use of the Spanish word, Manuel beamed. "*Sí!* Manuel and the señorita horse doctor—*amigos!*" Leigh tousled his black hair. "Thanks, Manuel. I could use a friend here."

TWO

The entrance to the ranch was marked by white-painted stucco columns. A wide graveled drive ran from the entrance about a half mile to the house. As soon as she had parked in the circular drive, Manuel opened the car door and hopped out.

"Thank you for the ride, señorita. I have to hurry."

Startled at his apparent eagerness to get away from her, Leigh asked, "Where is your house, Manuel?"

He pointed to a cluster of buildings several hundred yards to the south of the main house. A few of the structures, she saw, were white frame-houses; one of these was apparently where Manuel and his family lived.

"*Adiós, señorita,*" Manuel called as he leaped onto the grass and streaked away from her like a quick brown lizard.

Shaking her head, Leigh turned her attention to the ranch house. It was large and rambling, built in the Spanish style, its white stucco walls glistening in the sunlight. The lawn surrounding the house was immaculately groomed. Even now, sprinklers were wetting the thick, lush grass and shrubbery. Clumps of yucca and cactus were placed attractively about the lawn.

She stepped out of the car and straightened the waist-cinching blue skirt and tailored white blouse she wore. Both had been fresh and crisp when she'd started out that morning, but now they felt limp and rather damp.

She straightened her shoulders, and walked briskly along the curving cement walk that led to the front door.

A heavy black wrought-iron horse's head was fastened to one side of the massive front door with a ring underneath that served as a door knocker. Leigh lifted the ring, rapped several times, and waited.

Her knock was answered by a tall, raw-boned woman of about sixty, wearing a plain brown cotton dress and a white apron. Her pepper-and-salt hair was pulled back and wound in a knot on top of her head. She had light hazel eyes that regarded Leigh with mild curiosity.

"I'm Doctor Leigh Alexander."

The woman's expression changed to one of disbelief.

"I don't think I heard you rightly, miss. You don't mean to say you're Doctor Alexander, the new veterinarian, do you?"

"That's right," Leigh said with pretended self-assurance.

There was a split second when Leigh thought the woman was going to shut the door in her face, but then she recovered and stammered, "Come in, Doctor. I don't mean to keep you standing there in the heat. It's just that we—I mean, I didn't—"

"Expect a woman?" Leigh finished for her.

"Why, yes—that is, Mr. Casey failed to mention it."

Leigh stepped into a large, high-ceilinged foyer with a dark, tiled floor and white walls. The coolness of the air conditioning felt refreshing after the blazing sun outside.

"I'm Maggie Anderson," the woman was saying, "the housekeeper. You just call me Maggie. Everybody does."

She led Leigh into a book-lined study that opened off the foyer. "I'll go get Mr. Casey."

Too nervous to sit, Leigh wandered about the room, examining the paintings on the one wall which was not covered with bookshelves. One of them, she was almost certain, was a Charles Russell original. The others appeared to be originals, too, although the artist's name, scrawled in one corner, was unknown to her.

To her inexpert eye the paintings did have a flair. They were Mexican scenes, done in muted splashes of color that merely suggested figures and objects, as if the scenes were viewed through an expanse of water.

On another wall some of the shelves displayed horse show and racing trophies and several framed photographs of prize horses. The animals were fine specimens, and she itched to get her hands on them.

Restless again, she paced across to stand beside the dark polished desk that sat on a fringed Navaho rug. A covered portable typewriter stood on one side of the desk, and on the other, a wood base supported two gold penholders separated by a shining gold plaque engraved with the words: HAPPY BIRTHDAY, SHANE, DARLING. LOVE ALWAYS, PHYLLIS.

The study door opened suddenly and, startled, Leigh backed away from the desk, not wishing to be caught examining Shane Casey's personal belongings. The man who stood in the doorway was about thirty, dressed in jeans and a western shirt; he was tall and slender with dark hair and blue eyes that ran over her body from toes to shining hair. When his eyes met hers, one corner of his mouth lifted in a way that suggested he liked what he saw.

He shut the door and stood gazing across the room at her, a lazy grin spreading his lips wide. "Doctor Alexander, I presume."

Leigh was trying hastily to rearrange her image of Shane Casey. This man was not what she had expected at all. He was handsome and unexpectedly charming, and he didn't seem to be angry at discovering she was female, but somehow he was not as imposing nor as dynamic as she had expected Shane Casey to be.

"How do you do, Mr. Casey," she said, attempting to hide her surprise under a businesslike tone.

He crossed the room and perched on the side of the polished desk. "Since we'll be seeing a lot of each other, I suggest we drop the Mister and Doctor." His smile sought to put her at ease. "I'm Rod Casey, Leigh."

She was startled. "Oh, then you're not. . .?"

"Shane Casey? No, I'm his brother. Shane's gone to Kentucky to look at a horse, which is why he can't be here to welcome you. You'll have to make do with me for now."

"When is Mr. Casey due back?"

He lifted his shoulders. "Sometime tomorrow, I think, unless he decides to buy the horse, and then there will be long, drawn-out negotiations. My brother is very good at getting his money's worth. Which is why he's a millionaire, and I'm just a poor struggling rancher."

Leigh laughed, beginning to feel more at ease. She glanced about the handsomely appointed study. "I would hardly call this struggling."

"Oh, all of this—the house and everything in it—belongs to Shane."

"I'm sorry. I assumed the ranch was half yours."

He grinned easily. "The land is. Our father divided it equally between us at his death twelve years ago. In fact, I probably got the better part of the inheritance, since my half contained the old home-place, a two-story house, and several barns. Shane's half had only the hired hands' houses. After our father died, my brother went into hock up to his ears to buy his first quarter horses. It turned out he has an unfailing eye for a champion. Every horse he touches turns to money. He built this house eight years ago and"—he made a deprecating gesture with his hands—"the rest, as they say, is history."

"You live here with your brother?"

He nodded. "Shane's got Maggie and a couple of Mexican women who help her. It beats cooking my own meals and cleaning up after myself, and I make a little extra cash by renting out the old home-place. I also have some beef cattle. Unluckily I got into the cattle business when prices were high and, six months after I bought my herd, prices dropped. It took me three years to climb out of that hole." He lowered his eyes in what seemed to Leigh a flagrant bid for sympathy, but then he looked up and flashed a smile. "Aw, well. Easy come, easy go."

"You seem to take setbacks with good grace."

"Why not? Unlike Shane . . . I have always thought there are other things in life as important as making money." He hesitated. "From which you may gather that I'll never be as rich as my brother."

Leigh eyed him with amusement. "Don't expect any tears from me. Half of this ranch must be worth a great deal of money."

"On paper," he admitted. "But my father's will stipulated that neither Shane nor I could sell our share of the

24

ranch without the other's consent. My brother is adamant when it comes to hanging on to every inch of the land."

He seemed to expect some comment from her, but she remained silent and waited for him to say more. Before he could do so, a knock sounded at the study door.

"Mr. Rod." It was Maggie's voice. "I've got some iced tea and cookies ready for you and the doctor in the kitchen."

Rod got to his feet and went to the door. "Maggie, you're an angel."

"Sure, Mr. Rod," returned Maggie, "and I'll bet you say that to all the girls."

As Leigh followed him and the housekeeper along a long hall, he told her, "You will occupy a three-room apartment at the back of the house. Your predecessor," Rod went on, "Doctor Smith, stayed there while he was in my brother's employ. Smith took a government job and moved out about a month ago."

The kitchen was large and equipped with gleaming white appliances and every modern gadget one could imagine. There were two regular ovens and a microwave oven on one wall. Food processors, blenders, mixers and other small electrical appliances lined the shelves on another wall behind glass doors. A table and four chairs sat at one end in a small dining alcove, the walls of which were covered with bright-colored wallpaper depicting toreadors, flamenco dancers, and sleepy Mexican street scenes. The kitchen was a marvel of modern convenience, as well as being a bright, homey room. Leigh imagined that Maggie must enjoy working there.

A short, plump but pretty Mexican woman stood at a center island bar, chopping salad vegetables.

"Leigh," Rod said, "this is María Gomez, who helps Maggie with the cooking. María, this is our new veterinarian, Doctor Alexander."

María's brown eyes grew large, and a small giggle escaped her. "Hello, Doctor Alexander."

"Carmaleta, Maggie's other helper, has already gone home. You'll meet her tomorrow." Rod walked to the table and pulled out one of the kitchen chairs for her.

"Do you take sugar in your tea, Doctor?" Maggie asked.

"No," Leigh said. "And do you think you could call me Leigh? Doctor sounds so formal." She turned to María. "Mrs. Gomez, I think I met your son on the road from San Lorenzo. He was hitchhiking. I gave him a ride home."

"Manuel?" María shook her head, her dark eyes snapping. "I have told and told that boy not to hitchhike." She was suddenly struck by another thought and, glancing at the wall clock, she frowned. "It is now a little after three. What time did you pick up Manuel?"

"About two thirty," Leigh said. "Manuel said school let out early today."

"Ha!" María tossed the vegetable knife down on the cabinet top and swiped her plump hands across her apron.

Maggie carried two glasses of tea to the table. She gave María a sympathetic glance. "If you want to go down to the house for a few minutes, María, there will be time before dinner."

"*Gracias*," María said. "I'll go to the barn and get José. Manuel has played this little trick once too often. His father has warned him. . . ." She broke into a spate of Spanish, turned on her heel, and left the kitchen.

Manuel's eagerness to get away from Leigh at the front of the house now became understandable. He hadn't wanted his mother to see him.

Leigh saw Maggie's lips tighten. "It's his third year at that school, and he never played hookey until this year."

"It seems," Rod interrupted, "that Manuel and the third-grade teacher don't hit it off."

Maggie snatched up a damp dishcloth and began to wipe an already spotless counter top. "You have to have a little patience to work with children."

Rod chuckled. "Phyllis Calhoun has been known for a lot of things, but patience was never one of them."

Leigh recalled the "Love always, Phyllis" engraved on the pen holder on Shane Casey's desk. Was she the same Phyllis as Manuel's teacher?

The housekeeper's pale hazel eyes had darkened with

some strong emotion. "If you would be so good as to show Leigh to her quarters when you're done, Mr. Rod, I believe I'll lie down for a few minutes before starting dinner."

When the housekeeper had left them alone, Rod said lightly, "Maggie and Phyllis Calhoun don't hit it off any better than Phyllis and Manuel do."

"Why?" Leigh asked.

Rod shrugged and reached for another cookie. "Phyllis isn't the sort of woman other women take to. As for Manuel—well, that's another story, and too long and involved to go into now. If you're finished with your tea, I'll show you the apartment. Did you leave your luggage in your car?"

Leigh got to her feet. "Yes. It's parked out front."

"The garages are in back," he said as they left the kitchen. "I'll move it for you later if you like."

The apartment consisted of a living room, a bedroom, a small kitchen, and a bath. "Doctor Smith took most of his meals with the family," Rod told her. "Of course, you're welcome to do the same."

She shook her head. "Thank you, but I enjoy cooking." Besides, she thought, she must be very careful not to take anything for granted. Shane Casey was her employer and the owner of this house, not Rod. Any invitations to meals would have to come from him.

The apartment was neat and clean, furnished with pieces of heavy Spanish-style furniture. The walls were white and unadorned; the dark wood floors gleamed with wax and a few Navaho rugs, similar to the one in the study, were scattered about. It hardly looked as if it had ever been lived in, and Leigh imagined that Dr. Smith had spent as little time here as possible. She turned about on one heel, surveying the living room. The place had possibilities, though. She could pick up a few knickknacks and pictures for the walls. . . .

"I suspect, by the gleam in your eye," drawled Rod, "that you are imagining ruffles at all the windows and a big Persian cat curled up on the bed."

She laughed. "Not quite," and told herself to forget any

ideas of sprucing up the place. She said gravely, "This will do nicely."

Rod said with amusement, "It's not the Hilton. Originally, Shane planned this as living quarters for our aunt, but she died before the house was finished. I guess he lost interest after that."

"How do you think your brother is going to react to me?"

"I wouldn't care to speculate on that," he said judiciously, and then added, "but cheer up. I'm on your side. If you'll give me your car keys, I'll bring your luggage in for you and move your car."

When he left, she walked through the apartment again, imagining a picture here, a bright cushion there. She had never had a place of her own before. It would be fun to fix it up, even though she knew she would probably not have a chance to enjoy the fruits of her labor for long. She noticed that someone (Maggie?) had stocked the kitchen with enough groceries for a few days.

Rod soon returned with her luggage. "I insist that you make an exception this evening and have dinner with me. You must be tired after your long drive, too tired to cook. Actually you'll be doing me a favor. I dislike eating alone."

"All right," she agreed. "It's kind of you to ask me." She couldn't see what harm it could do, since Shane Casey was away.

"We'll eat about seven." He left then and Leigh spent the next hour unpacking her clothes and hanging them in the bedroom closet. Then, kicking off her shoes, she stretched out across the bed and fell asleep almost immediately.

She was brought back to consciousness by the sound of a car passing outside the bedroom window, its tires crunching on the gravel drive. When she glanced at her wristwatch, she saw it was six fifteen; she'd slept for over an hour.

Still yawning, she went into the bathroom and took a quick, rejuvenating shower. By the time she had applied a dash of makeup, brushed her hair, and dressed in casual

28

beige silk slacks and tunic, it was seven o'clock. She left the apartment, humming happily to herself as she went in search of the dining room, which she thought she had glimpsed through the kitchen doorway earlier.

She found it easily. It was large enough for a sizable banquet with the white walls common to the rest of the house, a cathedral ceiling, an enormous black wrought-iron chandelier. A lovely stained-glass window on the west was strewing the rays of the setting sun in bright patterns across the carpet.

The table setting was casual—bright-colored woven place-mats and a centerpiece of daisies. Surprisingly, however, three places of the heavy off-white pottery had been set.

Before she had a chance to puzzle long over the third place setting, Rod strolled into the room beside a dark-haired man, who eyed her without expression, which, for some reason, she found forbidding. But then he was a rather forbidding-looking man. It was more difficult to judge his age than Rod's, though she thought he must be in his middle thirties. He was stern-featured, his dark brows lowered over gray eyes which, at the moment, looked very steely indeed. He had a firm, straight nose which, in the muted light of the dining room, cast a soft shadow over the wide-lipped mouth below it. In spite of the feeling of foreboding that the man's presence had brought into the room, Leigh couldn't help wondering how that firm mouth would look if it should relax into a smile. She knew, of course, who the man was, even before Rod spoke—who he had to be. He was even more imposing than his pictures; more muscularly built and more darkly tanned than his brother. It had been his car that had awakened her.

"Leigh, my brother has returned from Kentucky earlier than expected. Shane, may I present Doctor Leigh Alexander."

She murmured an acknowledgement that Shane Casey did not deign to take note of; he spoke in a deep voice that gave no quarter to the niceties of polite conversation.

"You realize, of course, that we did not expect a girl."

Straight to the heart of the matter, thought Leigh,

rather like a dagger. But in the face of those penetrating gray eyes, she felt a need to dissemble. "From your housekeeper's and your brother's reactions earlier today, I suspected that was the case. I regret that Professor Harlan didn't tell you."

The silence that met this statement was palpable. Glancing from Shane Casey's face to his brother's, she saw one expression of impatient disbelief and another of amusement.

"I had hoped," she went on, "that my sex would not be considered relevant to my employment. If I had known that a preujdice against women existed here, I would have refused to come."

"It's a little late now to dwell on what you might have done but did not do," Shane Casey said. "We must reach an agreement as to what is to be done now. In my opinion, the best thing for all concerned, is for you to return to Oklahoma and accept another job offer. I will, of course, pay you a month's salary for the inconvenience the trip may have caused you."

"What about the three months trial I was guaranteed?"

"Under the circumstances, I would prefer to retract that offer," he said without a hint of embarrassment or regret. "If you insist, I may be obliged to pay you the full three months salary for your trouble."

"I have no desire to take money for services I have not performed." Leigh squared her shoulders and stretched herself to her full height which, even in the high wedges she wore, was several inches less than Shane Casey's six-feet-plus of solid substance. As she did so, the clinging fabric of her tunic molded more prominently to the full contours of her breast. She was aware of this because her movement had attracted Rod's attention, and his gaze had settled on her blouse, the blue eyes suddenly glinting with alertness.

"I was under the impression you were a man of your word, Mr. Casey," she said. "At least, that is what my guardian told me."

"Your guardian?" Shane Casey queried.

"Professor Harlan became my guardian six years ago

when my parents were killed in a car crash. Knowing my desire to work with horses, he urged me to accept your offer. Evidently he had enough faith in my abilities to feel that in three months I could live up to your high standards."

"One needs more than a romanticized idea of horses to care for high-strung racers such as I raise, Doctor Alexander," he said condescendingly. "It requires physical strength, as well as skill."

Irritated, she stared across the room at him and wished she did not feel so young in her casual attire, her long tresses tumbling about her shoulders.

"More skill than strength," she said. "I've been associated with horses since I was ten, and I specialized in their care at the university."

"How many racehorses have you handled?" he asked. Seeing her expression, his lips curved slightly in what, Leigh supposed, was intended to be a smile, although the gray eyes remained aloof. "You also have to be more stubborn than my horses, Doctor Alexander, and that is very stubborn indeed. But perhaps you *do* qualify in that respect."

"You have to admit, Shane, she's a spunky little thing." Rod Casey dragged his gaze away from the front of her blouse and smiled at her. But the smile faded when he saw her frown. "Hey, Leigh, that was a compliment."

"It may surprise you to learn," she said scathingly, "that being called 'spunky' isn't my idea of a compliment." She turned her gaze on Shane Casey. "Nor do I think being considered more stubborn than your horses any great shakes. I am a competent veterinarian. I've been well trained and I expect nothing more than to be allowed to do my job. I wish to be judged on professional merit alone, just like any man."

"Evidently Doctor Alexander learned to stand up for her rights at the university too." Shane Casey spoke in a tone that indicated that he did not consider this a particularly desirable trait in the present instance. "A truly liberated woman, it would appear."

Since she suspected he was trying to goad her into some

31

sort of emotional outburst, Leigh did not give him the satisfaction of responding.

"Aren't you being a little hard on her?" Rod said.

"I don't ask or expect any special favors," Leigh said at once. "I wish to be treated as you treated Doctor Smith."

"I doubt that you appreciate all the implications of that," Shane Casey said dryly. "But since you've called my word into question, I feel obligated—against my better judgment—to honor it. You shall have your three months trial, if you insist, Doctor Alexander."

"When do I start?" she asked quickly, so as not to give him another opportunity to back down.

"Tomorrow morning at nine. I'll meet you at the horse barn. Does that suit you?" His tone was cool.

"Perfectly." Her tone was equally cool. "I'll be there."

"I have a man—José Gomez—who feeds and exercises the horses and keeps their stalls clean. Do you wish me to assign another of the hired hands to help you handle the horses when José is occupied elsewhere?"

She knew at once that to say yes would make him think she was unsure of her ability; and to say no might lead to a few difficult situations in the beginning. However, she had no choice. "I won't need any special help." What a conceited, detestable man he was! She did not find it difficult to believe he had made himself a millionaire in the space of a few years. He was undoubtedly ruthless.

"Shall we be seated then?" Shane Casey said blandly.

Maggie entered the room at that moment, which made Leigh suspect she had been listening outside the door for the proper time to serve, and she must have heard the entire conversation.

"Well, Shane, what about the horse you went to see?" Rod said, turning the focus on the conversation away from Leigh, for which she was grateful.

"The owner was asking too much for him," Shane said.

During the remainder of the meal Rod and Shane discussed horses, freeing Leigh from the necessity of making many comments. She was glad when dessert was finished and she could excuse herself to return to her apartment.

But she hadn't reached her door when Rod Casey caught up with her.

"What's your hurry? I was hoping for a chance to talk to you alone so we could get better acquainted. Would you like to go for a drive?"

"Thank you, but no," Leigh said. "I have some letters to write, and I want to get to bed early before my first day on the job."

"Leigh, we're going to be living here together. It'll be much more pleasant if we can all be friends."

"I can't picture your brother being friendly."

"Don't let him get under your skin. Finding out you're a woman took him unawares. I'd given him the news only a few minutes before we came into the dining room. Besides, he's used to having his own way about everything."

This gave Leigh another reason for disliking Shane Casey. How typical of a man like him to be rude when things didn't go exactly as planned. "How fortunate for him," she said with irony. "Few people are in such an enviable position."

"If you won't go for a drive tonight," Rod persisted, "how about having dinner with me in San Lorenzo tomorrow night? It's just a wide spot in the road, but there is one pretty good Mexican restaurant."

"I'll have to see how I feel tomorrow," Leigh demurred. "For the first few days, I expect I'll be putting in some long hours." She had no intention of giving Shane Casey the smallest cause for complaint.

Rod did not try to persuade her further, and she entered the bare living room of the apartment with relief at being finally alone. She had told Uncle Jess that all she wanted was a chance to prove herself, and now she had it. Perhaps, she thought now, she ought to give Shane Casey a chance too. She wanted to be fair, and although she had already started to form an opinion of her employer, she was determined not to let it interfere with her work; it was not necessary to like the man to be a good employee.

As for Rod Casey, he was charming and easy to be with . . . but she had seen him turn that same charm on Maggie and no doubt he used it on all females. It meant very little and probably was a poor indicator of his true thoughts. Besides, Rod, no matter how charming, had no say in how long she could keep her job here. At least with his brother she knew exactly where she stood.

THREE

At a quarter of nine the next morning, Leigh, in jeans and a cotton shirt, her long hair secured in back with a large clasp, arrived at the horse barn. It was a huge, corrugated steel structure with holding pens and corrals spreading out from it on two sides. Inside a number of stalls ran along one wall, although all but one of them were empty now; the horses were probably allowed out to pasture in good weather. Leigh stood at the open barn door, inhaling the pungent odor of horses. She had never found the smell unpleasant, as some of her girl friends had. Her eyes grew accustomed to the dimness within, and she made her way to the one stall that was closed. A slight Mexican man stood as she approached. She hadn't seen him before. He had been lounging against the stall gate—sleeping, Leigh guessed, because now he covered a yawn with one hand.

"Good morning," Leigh greeted him.

"You are Doctor Alexander? Señor Shane told me to expect you. He'll be here soon. I'm José Gomez. I'll be helping you with the horses."

Leigh extended her hand. "I've already met your wife and son, and I've looked forward to meeting you, José."

He grinned and shook her hand, his teeth flashing white in the dimness. "Have you been waiting long?" Leigh asked.

"I've been here most of the night. Lady, one of the mares, is not well."

"I'd like to take a look at her."

He hesitated for only a moment, but in that moment she could see that he was having difficulty imagining her being of much help to Lady. "I will go in first," he said as

35

he reached for the handle on the stall gate. "She is nervous with strangers, and it's worse when she's sick."

Leigh followed the Mexican man into the stall, where a large ceiling-light burned.

"Stay near the gate until she gets used to you," José warned.

Leigh obeyed, and José walked toward the beautiful chestnut mare, talking soothingly. After a few minutes he took hold of the mare's halter and led her toward Leigh. Lady limped on one front leg. Leigh stroked the mare's neck and talked to her for several minutes. "She has a fever," she told José. She kept stroking and talking while she bent to look at the leg Lady was favoring. "That boil on her leg will have to be lanced."

"I feared so," José said sadly. "I was hoping it would go away without using the knife. I don't like to make her pain worse."

Leigh smiled at his genuine concern for the mare. She liked this small, wiry Mexican man. "It will hurt worse for only a moment, and then it will feel much better."

"I am sure you are right," José admitted. "Come, I will show you where we keep the medical supplies."

A narrow computer with cabinets above it had been built along part of one wall of the barn. Supplies and medicines were jumbled together on the shelves in no apparent order, and dust had accumulated on the counter top. Everything would have to be cleaned and organized, Leigh saw. She shuffled through the supplies until she found a scalpel and a small pan. José filled the pan with water from the faucet over the sink built into one end of the counter and set it on a hot plate to boil. Leigh scrubbed the scalpel with disinfectant, then dropped it into the pan of boiling water. "She should have an antibiotic too," she said to José.

"I think Doctor Smith ordered some not long before he left." José rummaged until he found an unopened bottle of milky-white liquid.

Leigh examined the label. "That'll do fine." She found a syringe with a hypodermic needle and added it to the boiling water. Then she found a well-used pair of rubber gloves, a bottle of alcohol for cleaning the infected area, and a nearly empty jar of salve.

Finally they returned to the stall and José held firmly to Lady's halter, crooning to her while Leigh cleansed the boil and lanced it with one swift, sure movement. The mare snorted and tried to throw her head back, but José calmed her, and after a moment she allowed Leigh to press some of the poison from the cut and apply a layer of thick yellow salve. Lady suffered the injection of the antibiotic with only a whinny and Leigh stroked the mare's neck, saying, "There, girl. You'll feel a lot better now."'

Suddenly, without warning, Lady snorted and threw her head up, jerking free from José's grasp. "Down, girl, down!" José commanded sternly. Lady's nostrils flared and her eyes rolled. In a flash she reared up on her hind legs. Leigh backed away.

"Get out of there!" Leigh hadn't known that Shane Casey was standing at the open gate until he took hold of her wrist and pulled her out of the stall. Inside, José continued to talk to Lady, calming her.

"Why didn't you wait until I was here to help you?" Shane demanded. He glared down at her from his towering height, his thick brows drawn together in anger, the line of his jaw hard and jutting. His plaid shirt was open at the neck, revealing a triangle of dark, curling hair. Leigh felt suddenly weak at being so close to the hard maleness of this man, who seemed determined to dislike her.

She pulled away, stripping off the rubber gloves and facing him squarely. "I didn't think I needed your help."

"Obviously you were wrong."

"I don't think so," said Leigh stubbornly. "She's in pain, but she allowed me to lance the boil and give her an injection. You're overreacting."

"I won't have you injured by one of my horses!"

"Did you feel you had to protect Doctor Smith?"

"You know very well I didn't. He knew what he was doing."

"That's my point," said Leigh indignantly. "I know what I'm doing, too, and I'd appreciate it if you'd let me do it."

"I knew this was a mistake!" Shane whirled on one boot heel and stalked across the barn.

José thrust his head out of the stall then, grinning sheepishly in his embarrassment at overhearing the argument between Leigh and his employer. "Do you think it would be all right to turn her into one of the holding pens?"

"Yes," Leigh said. "The fresh air will be good for her."

José led the limping mare from the stall, through the barn, and out the back door.

Leigh went to the sink and scrubbed her hands, ignoring Shane, who leaned against the counter, watching her. She dried her hands on a paper towel and turned to her employer. "I think the first order of business is to clean up these cabinets and make a list of needed supplies."

His gray eyes assessed her coolly. "You're wondering how things got in such a mess, aren't you?"

"Frankly, yes. I've never seen a vet's things in quite such a muddle before."

He shrugged, straightening to his full height, his muscular legs in the tight jeans spread slightly. "Doctor Smith had a drinking problem. I kept him longer than I should have, hoping he'd come out of it. Finally I had no choice but to let him go. He got a job with the government where he'll be under constant supervision. I think he'll be able to handle his problem better under those circumstances." He gestured toward the cluttered cabinets. "The last few months he was here, he did very little."

Leigh didn't know what to say, feeling she had been too self-righteous in her scorn of her predecessor. "I didn't mean to criticize him."

He grinned, and his eyes raked over her insolently. She felt her cheeks grow warm and was glad for the dimness on this side of the barn. "Remember last night when you said you wanted me to treat you exactly as I treated Doctor Smith, and I said you didn't understand all the implications of that?"

She nodded, wondering what he was getting at and sensing, somehow, that he was enjoying her discomfort.

"I was thinking that I frequently had to undress him and put him to bed at night."

Leigh felt the warmth in her cheeks spread down her neck, and she looked away, unable to meet his teasing gaze. "I'd better get busy here." She began to take things from one of the cabinets.

Finally he said, "I thought we'd saddle a couple of horses and ride over the ranch this afternoon."

"Fine."

There was a pause, then he said, "Look, Leigh, I'm sorry I lost my temper a while ago. It's just that I'd had so much trouble with Smith, and then you showed up and—"

Indignation overcame her embarrassment. She turned to glare at him. "And you couldn't decide which was worse, a drunk or a female. Right?"

He threw his head back and laughed. "You just looked like you ought to be lounging beside a swimming pool with a cool mint julep in your hand instead of taking care of horses."

"Appearances can be deceiving," she retorted. "Not that pool-lounging isn't a pleasant enough pastime. But I couldn't make a career of it."

"I know several women who have."

"Then I feel sorry for them."

He slanted a quizzical look at her. "Some of them are married to friends of mine. Don't let them hear you say that. They can be vicious when they feel their dignity has been insulted, vicious in a way that only women can be."

She studied his features surreptitiously from beneath half-lowered lashes. She found herself thinking that it was a strong face, in a hard sort of way, as well as an attractive one. The face of a man who would take charge in any circumstance. If she had been his mother or the elderly aunt Rod had mentioned, she would have trusted him implicitly. But she was equally as certain that it would be folly for a young woman to do so. From his remark about the wives of his friends, he didn't appear to hold most women in very high regard. "I am not likely ever to come into contact with your friends and their wives."

"On the contrary. I'll be entertaining several times during the summer."

"Don't tell me the hired help are included in the guest list."

"You aren't exactly in the same category as house servants and hired hands. Doctor Smith was a frequent guest at my parties, as well as those of my friends. I'm certain a young, attractive, unattached woman like you will not go unnoticed by our neighborhood society." His lip curled around the last word, as if he were making fun. "You *are* unattached, aren't you?"

"Completely."

His expression was curious. She thought he wanted to draw more from her about her personal life, probably hoping she might be expected to marry at any moment and leave her post here. But he only said, "Surely you don't intend to spend all your time pursuing your career."

"I expect it will take most of my time. In the beginning, anyway."

He shook his head as if he couldn't fathom her motives. He started toward an enclosed area at the far corner of the barn. "I'm going to get caught up on some horse records in my office here. If you need me, call." He went into the paneled cubicle and closed the door behind him.

Leigh looked at the closed door for a moment, wishing he would return to his study at the house to work on the records. The idea of his being only a few yards away while she worked gave her an uncomfortable feeling. Acknowledging this, she felt bewildered. What was it about Shane Casey that could make her feel like a gauche adolescent again?

This is silly and extremely unprofessional, she told herself angrily. Pushing thoughts of her enigmatic employer aside, she turned to the task at hand. During the next two hours, she forgot all about Shane Casey. She emptied the overhead cabinets and scrubbed them with hot water and disinfectant. Then she organized the medicines and supplies so that she could find whatever she needed at a moment's notice. As she worked she jotted down missing items and those in short supply on a tablet she had found

40

in one of the drawers. She was soon perspiring, and her hands were smudged with dirt. Occasionally a long strand of hair slipped free of the confining clasp and fell across her face. Intent upon the work, she absentmindedly smoothed each loose strand away from her face as it fell, and tucked it back into the clasp. The fact that her face was becoming dust-streaked did not even occur to her because she was fully occupied with what were, to her, more important matters.

Shortly before noon Shane Casey emerged from the cubicle office. Engrossed as she was, Leigh was not, at first, aware of him, which gave him a chance to study her at work. What he saw bewildered and, in some way, irritated him. The slender blond girl, with the unlikely title of Doctor of Veterinary Medicine, moved with unconscious grace and an energy that surprised him. There was a wide, dark streak across one cheek and a smudge on the end of her pert nose; her shirt and jeans were grimy from frequent swipes of her small, dirty hands. To add to the disheveled look, her cotton shirt, damp with perspiration, molded the curves of her breasts and clung to her narrow back. It was this that disconcerted him most.

Enclosed in the coolness of the small office, where a window air-conditioning unit had been installed, he'd forgotten how stuffy and hot the barn could become in the summer heat. A large rotary fan was built into the barn loft on one end and would have at least provided a breeze. But Leigh could not have known about the fan, and he hadn't thought to mention it to her. He felt a flash of unreasoning anger. Whether at himself for the oversight or at her for not complaining, he couldn't tell. Whatever its source, it caused him to sound brusque when he spoke.

"There's a fan in here. The switch is over on that wall."

Her preoccupation shattered, she turned to face him. She felt dirty and sticky and tired. She regarded his impatient scowl with ill-concealed resentment as she swiped at the perspiration on her forehead, leaving another dark streak. "I wish I'd known that earlier."

He strode toward her. "I don't know what you're trying

to prove, but you don't have to do this kind of manual labor. I told you I'd assign another man to help you."

Her ire now kindled, she snapped back, "And I told you I don't need any help."

He towered over her, his gray eyes narrowing. "Did you finish here?"

She took a step back, flustered at the glint of fire in his eyes. "No," she said weakly. His nearness made her embarrassingly aware of how the sweat-drenched shirt hugged her body. Then, determined not to appear disquieted, she rushed on, "I haven't even started on the lower cabinets, and the refrigerator has to be scrubbed from top to bottom. I can probably finish it tomorrow."

"José will help you."

"That isn't necessary. I don't want—"

The oath he uttered silenced her momentarily. "My God, you are stubborn! *I* am the boss here. José will help you!"

She fought down an impulse to argue further. "Whatever you say, Mr. Casey."

He thrust his hands into his jeans pockets, as if not trusting himself not to shake her. "Will you get off your high horse? My name is Shane."

"I am attempting," she retorted coolly, "to keep things on a professional level."

He uttered an impatient growl. "We all live too close together here for formality. Besides, don't expect me to look at you like *this*"—his glance raked over her, a sneer pulling at his mouth—"and call you Doctor."

The words Leigh would have liked to offer in response to that insult trembled on her tongue. But she was learning self-restraint. She would *not* allow this pompous, egotistical man to goad her into a verbal duel. Partly, she realized with dismay, because she had no chance of winning such a contest.

Trying to appear unruffled, she glanced at her watch. "If you will excuse me, it's lunchtime." She turned and walked toward the barn door.

"I'll meet you here at two for our ride over the ranch," he called after her.

She didn't break stride as she replied, "I'll be here." Then she was outside, and she hurried toward the main house.

In her apartment she looked at her reflection in the bathroom mirror, realizing that her appearance had been even more bedraggled than she had feared during the latest confrontation with her employer. She undressed quickly and stepped into the shower, already beginning to dread the afternoon's ride.

Promptly at two she was back at the horse barn, clean jeans tucked into riding boots and paired with a cool, scoop-neck knit shirt. She had pinned her hair into a prim knot at the back of her head, and she hoped she managed to appear aloofly confident as she swung herself into the saddle of the horse José held for her.

Shane was mounted on a spirited black stallion. Leigh's horse was a more sedate chestnut gelding named Skipper. The gelding, Shane explained, was a son of Lady, the mare Leigh had treated that morning, who had not proved himself as a racer and had, therefore, been relegated to the more mundane position as dependable mount for guests at the ranch who wished to ride. He would be available for Leigh to ride, Shane said, whenever she needed him. Leigh stroked the gelding's neck companionably as they started out, feeling a kinship with the horse who, like Leigh herself, had failed to live up to the master's expectations.

"Maggie set a place for you at lunch," Shane said as the horses settled into a comfortable gait.

"I explained to Rod that I prefer preparing my own meals."

Shane darted a quizzical look at her, then shrugged carelessly. "As you wish."

She started to explain that she hadn't wanted to appear presumptuous, but the square set of his jaw silenced her. He seemed determined to find fault, no matter what she said.

"I think Rod hoped you'd change your mind," he went on after a moment. "He mentioned something about plans

43

for the evening." He seemed to find Rod's disappointment interesting.

"Your brother invited me out to dinner tonight," she explained stiffly, although why she felt compelled to explain anything to him was beyond her understanding.

"Never let it be said," remarked Shane wryly, "that Rod lets any grass grow under his feet." His long glance in her direction was assessing, as if, contrary to his words, he thought she might have somehow taken advantage of his brother. This suspicion angered her, particularly when she remembered how studiously charming and persistent Rod had been. Besides, what business was it of Shane's how she spent her off-hours, and with whom? Undecided until then about whether to accept Rod's invitation, she found, in that moment, that she intended to say yes, merely because something in Shane Casey's manner seemed disapproving.

"Rod was very hospitable to me yesterday."

His eyebrows shot up. "I see." She did not know what he meant by that, and she felt sure she didn't want to know. She changed the subject abruptly. "Tomorrow I should have completed the list of supplies we'll be needing. I thought, if you like, I could drive into San Antonio on Saturday and get them."

They had taken a trail that wound away from the barn in a southeasterly direction. Glancing back, Leigh saw that the ranch buildings were lost from sight behind a gently sloping rise in the land. Her gaze swept to either side, finding no other houses, only far-spreading green pastures, and she was impressed by the obvious size of the Casey Ranch.

As if he could read her thoughts, Shane, who had pulled slightly ahead, called back, "We have about twenty thousand acres enclosed. Another few hundred acres are worthless for grazing purposes, so we haven't bothered fencing them." They were approaching a wide gate ahead, and with one lithe movement he swung his long body to the ground. He opened the gate, pushing it aside as he led the stallion through, and waited for Leigh to follow before he secured the gate once more.

He swung back into his saddle. "Most of the two-year-olds are in this pasture." He spurred the stallion to a gallop and Leigh urged her gelding to catch up. When they were riding side by side again, he returned to her earlier comment. "Except in cases of emergency, your weekends are your own. I don't expect you to spend them running ranch errands."

"Oh, I don't mind," she assured him. "I'd planned to go into San Antonio, anyway—to see an old friend. As long as I'll be there, I might as well pick up the supplies."

"I'm going to San Antonio myself Saturday," he said. "You can ride in with me. I'll be returning Saturday evening." He looked inquiringly at her. "Unless you planned to spend the night."

Incredibly she felt herself blushing. Why did she insist upon reading double meanings into everything he said? He couldn't possibly know that her "old friend" was a man. And yet something in the glint of his gray eyes told her he did. "No, I won't be spending the night." She cast about in search of some excuse, any excuse, to decline his offer of transportation to San Antonio. She could find none that did not sound like a blatant falsehood.

Shane indicated a dark herd beneath a cluster of trees in the distance. "We'll go this way."

Leigh nodded, pushing back a stray wisp of hair. She shaded her eyes with her hand, then reined Skipper to follow Shane's broad back.

"I should have reminded you to bring a hat," he said as she rode abreast. "My skin is accustomed to the sun, but you're going to have a peeling nose, I'm afraid."

Leigh's attention was on the horses, who were resting near a pond in the shade of a line of oak trees. As they drew nearer, the animals' fine breeding was obvious in their massive chests and muscular hindquarters. These horses were bred for quick starts and speed over short distances. "Have you raced any of these?"

He nodded. "Regionally. My top racers are in another pasture closer to the barn. José checks them twice a day. We'll circle around that way if there's time before returning to the house."

Leigh forgot her former discomfort with this man as she listened attentively to his detailing of the bloodlines and

45

show and racing performances of the horses before them. They were fine specimens, and she wished, with a pang, that she had longer than three months to care for them.

"These are on a regular vaccination schedule. I think Doctor Smith left records, of a sort, in the desk in the barn office. You might look for them when you have time. Smith wasn't much of a record-keeper, and I'm afraid that's essential where proof of breeding and scheduled care is so important."

They left the pasture to pass through another containing mares and colts. Leigh smiled at the spindly-legged youngsters wobbling along beside their mothers. "They're beautiful!" she exclaimed.

Shane indicated a particularly spritely palomino colt. "That one's out of Fame and Fortune, the Ruidoso Downs winner three years ago. The dam's had two Hot Springs winners, both sired by other horses. I have high hopes for him."

They left that pasture, continuing in a wide circle that would eventually lead them back to the pasture where the ranch's top racers were penned, and beyond that to the horse barn.

The remainder of their ride passed quickly as Shane expanded upon future plans for various horses. The shows, the races—names that were only vaguely familiar to Leigh—rolled off his tongue effortlessly. He knew his business and his horses intimately. By five o'clock, when they returned to the barn, Leigh had begun to feel almost at ease with her employer.

But this feeling seemed to disappear like a wisp of summer cloud as they entered one of the corrals. Shane dismounted and tossed the stallion's reins over a hitching post, then turned and strode toward Leigh. Belatedly, she realized he was coming to help her dismount. Why this should disconcert her she didn't know, but she felt the racing of her pulse as he approached, looking up at her through dark lashes that were narrowed to filter the bright sunlight. She didn't want him to treat her like a—*woman*! In her anxiety, she was not even aware of the irrationality of that thought. She was perfectly capable of getting off a

46

horse on her own. And she would prove it—before he reached her.

In her haste, however, she miscalculated the position of the stirrup and almost fell when she swung down. A hand reached out and caught her by the arm and she was, at the same time, grateful and perturbed by the strength and assurance in the fingers that steadied her.

"There's no need for haste." The deep voice was tinged with mockery. "I never bite female veterinarians. Except by invitation."

Leigh was mortified, aware that she would have fallen if he hadn't caught her. She tried to break free of his grip, but his fingers remained clamped about her slender upper arm. She had to stand there and submit to the scrutiny of his eyes as they riveted her own, making her more aware than ever before of the iron strength of this man's will. Every inch of her resented him—for the taunt in his narrowed eyes and for the unnerving effect his overpowering maleness had on her. No man had the right to be so arrogantly sure of himself, as if no woman had ever dared contest his dominance.

Then his free hand moved to brush falling strands of blond hair from her face, lingering on her brow in what was almost a caress. "Your nose is going to peel, all right." Then he laughed, deliberately raking his gray eyes over her face and the bare neck of her shirt. "How old are you, Leigh?"

"Twenty-four," she said defiantly. "Why?"

"You blush like a teen-age virgin. I believe you are a member of a vanishing breed—a chaste woman." He scowled then and let her go. "So you had best be on guard against my brother tonight."

Leigh felt the blood leave her face and her hand itched to slap his face—so darkly superior it seemed, glistening with fine beads of perspiration like tiny diamond chips.

"You really are a—a cad, aren't you?" She struggled to find the most descriptive word, unaware that her choice of the old-fashioned term made her seem even younger and more naive.

He smiled, enjoying her inability to put him in his

47

place. "Probably. At least, when compared to elderly professors and callow students. But isn't it about time you grew up, Leigh? There is no Professor Harlan here to take care of you."

"I can take care of myself." Leigh couldn't keep a note of despair out of her voice.

"I hope so. In the event you discover you have overestimated your ability, you can always resign."

"Y-you think you can force me to leave, don't you?"

Leigh turned her head away and glanced toward the dark interior of the barn behind Shane. Where was José?

Seeing the direction of her gaze, Shane said, "José will take care of the horses in a little while."

"Let me pass, please," she said. "I don't want anyone to see us and get the wrong idea. You aren't dealing with Phyllis now."

"What did you say?" The words came swiftly, edged with anger. What in the world had made her utter that name, the name engraved on the penholder in his study? Mortification at her faux pas seemed to paralyze her.

Then the sound of a door slamming inside the barn reached them, and José's voice called out, "You have given the horses a good workout, Señor Shane." The Mexican man appeared in the doorway, smiling.

Leigh edged her way past Shane and slipped into the barn. Then, almost running, she crossed the interior and emerged in the sunlight on the other side. She made for the house, glancing back over her shoulder once as she neared the yard. Shane Casey was walking in the same direction as she, but more slowly. His tanned face was unreadable. She felt a stab of humiliation at the remembered conversation in the corral and caught her bottom lip between her teeth in consternation.

Now she would look forward to Saturday with trepidation. Was there no escaping Shane Casey's unnerving presence, even on the weekends?

FOUR

"I'm sorry I couldn't get away sooner. I wanted to drive into San Antonio." Rod Casey looked across the table at Leigh, his blue eyes truly apologetic, as if he feared she would not approve of this simple little restaurant in San Lorenzo with its checked tablecloths and uncarpeted floors.

Leigh glanced around the small dining room. Only about half the tables were occupied, and fully half of the diners were Mexican. None of the men, Leigh noticed, wore suits or even ties. She smoothed the skirt of her yellow cotton dress, glad that Rod had warned her to wear something casual. "It smells heavenly in here, so the food has to be good," she told him.

"It is," he agreed. "Plain, but tasty. The atmosphere may leave something to be desired, but I doubt we could find better Mexican food, even in San Antonio."

A waitress appeared and Leigh said, "Why don't you order for both of us."

Rod leered suggestively. "You trust me, eh? That may come in handy later."

Leigh laughed and said pointedly, "Don't count on it."

Rod frowned and turned his attention to the menu. "We'll have the *Pozole, tamales de elote,* and *atole champurrado*." He looked across at Leigh. "Would you like to try their special coffee? It's probably the most authentic thing on the menu. I've tasted coffee very like it in Mexico City."

She nodded and he added *café de la olla* to their order.

As the waitress left he said, "I have a number of heifers dropping first calves. One of them delivered this afternoon,

49

which is why I was late getting back to the house to clean up."

"Stop apologizing," Leigh said. "I understand. By the way, they're doing research with a new drug at Oklahoma State. It seems to help first-calf heifers have easier deliveries. I'll get some information on it for you, if you like."

"I'd appreciate that." He grinned and added, "I've never had a conversation like this with a dinner date before."

She acknowledged the humor in his remark, then said, "I'm just as glad we didn't have time to drive far. I find I'm extremely tired."

Rod grimaced. "Shane can be a slave driver. Don't let him take advantage of you."

Her answering smile was thoughtful, as she wondered whether his advice was meant professionally or personally—or both. She found it ironic that each of the Casey brothers had felt it necessary to warn her about the other. "As a matter of fact, he was angry with me for attacking that mess in the barn on my own. He insisted upon assigning José to help me tomorrow."

"I see." Rod toyed with a dinner fork while Leigh sipped from her water glass and became aware of the glances of curiosity from two young women seated at a nearby table.

She leaned forward and asked in a low voice, "Who are those women at the corner table?"

He glanced toward the table she indicated and, smiling, waved a greeting. "Two of San Lorenzo's schoolteachers, The redhead is Phyllis Calhoun. She's a—uh—friend of Shane's."

Leigh could not comment immediately, for just then the waitress brought their meal. Remembering Shane's electric reaction when she mentioned the redhead's name, however, she couldn't help being curious about her.

They sampled the tamales. "Mmm, delicious!" Leigh exclaimed. "This Phyllis Calhoun," she went on, after a moment, "is she also Manuel's teacher?"

"The same," drawled Rod. "Phyllis is from Dallas. Her father's very well-off. One of those rags-to-riches stories.

50

He made his money in the oil business. Papa's convinced he appreciates his wealth more because he knows what it is to be poor, to have to work for modest wages. He insisted that Phyllis and her older brother finish college and work for a living. The brother was a very low-echelon executive for a construction company for five years before he was allowed to go into the family business."

"That explains why Phyllis is teaching school," Leigh commented. "But not why she chose a small town like San Lorenzo."

Rod chuckled. "Our Phyllis is not very subtle, I'm afraid. She found a position as close to Shane as she could get."

"She knew him before she came here?"

"Oh, we've known the Calhouns for years. My father and old man Calhoun had business dealings. Also, Shane is on every Texas society matron's list of eligible bachelors, and Dallas society is among the most glittering. He's invited to some sort of social gathering there several times a year as, of course, is Phyllis."

"Is she a good teacher?"

Her question seemed to surprise Rod, and plainly he found it amusing. "Probably not. Her dedication is entirely focused in another direction. She is determined to marry Shane."

Leigh didn't know why she found this idea unacceptable. "Will she succeed, do you think?"

He shrugged. "Who knows? They make a good pair, in my opinion. They are both selfish and proud—and relentless when it comes to getting what they want. Phyllis just might be the woman to snag Shane, although he has never shown any interest in marriage up to now." He sipped his coffee, watching her over the rim. "Shane is a man who enjoys variety in his women. Marriage might cramp his style a bit."

Shocked by this sardonic assessment of his brother's character, Leigh sought to remain noncommittal. She did not wish to be guilty of criticizing her employer, regardless of how much she might agree with Rod. As inexperienced as she was in business, she was still shrewd enough to realize it would be most unwise to be found biting the hand that feeds one. "On the afternoon of my arrival," she ventured, "I got the impression that Manuel didn't like school. I wonder if the teacher has had to clamp down on him because he's a discipline problem."

Rod regarded her with intent blue eyes. "I don't think discipline has anything to do with it. Manuel went through the first two grades without a complaint from school."

Leigh sampled her coffee thoughtfully. It was sweet with a slight cinnamon flavor that she found pleasant. "What could be Manuel's problem then?"

"Phyllis has sent several notes home with the boy. She says he's slow and has even mentioned putting him in a learning-disabled class."

Leigh frowned. "But isn't that a class for retarded children?"

"I'm not sure." His expression was puzzled. "Why should it matter to you? You've only seen the boy once, haven't you?"

Absently Leigh pushed the remains of her meal about on her plate with her fork. "Yes, but he seemed extremely bright to me. I can't believe he's mentally retarded."

"Perhaps," said Rod, and his eyelids lowered, giving him a hooded. secret look, "putting Manuel in the special class will get him out of Phyllis's sight. Apparently his mere presence irritates her. School closes in a week, and something will have to be decided before next term. San Lorenzo's school population is so small that most of the teachers are responsible for two grade-levels. If Manuel is passed on to the regular fourth-grade class, he'd be assigned to Phyllis for another term."

Leigh stared at him. "Manuel is one of the sweetest, most charming children I've ever met. Why should Phyllis Calhoun dislike him?"

"I don't pretend to understand what motivates Phyllis."

Leigh knew, somehow, that he could have told her more but, for reasons of his own, had decided against it. "It would be a shame to erroneously brand a child as retarded, don't you agree?"

His response was indifferent. "Most of our rural Mexican-Americans don't finish high school, anyway."

Leigh bristled and had to fight to keep her voice lowered to a conversational level. As it was, her tone had a decidedly sarcastic edge. "So just write Manuel off, is that what you're suggesting?"

He gave her a hurt look. "Don't blame me, Leigh. If you must champion Manuel's cause, talk to Shane."

"Why should I talk to your brother?"

"He's a member of the school board. They don't transfer a child to a learning-disabled class solely on the teacher's say-so. There must be hard evidence, a battery of test scores. And the parents and school board have to agree with the teacher."

"It seems so unfair to poor Manuel," she persisted.

"Lots of things aren't fair, Leigh. Why, for example, should Shane be allowed to keep me from selling my part of the ranch?"

When she did not reply, he inquired abruptly, "Would you like dessert, or another cup of coffee?"

"Just coffee."

He signaled the waitress and she approached, filled their cups, and moved to another table.

"Rod! I *thought* it was you."

Startled, Leigh looked up to see a curvaceous, red-haired woman standing beside their table. Phyllis Calhoun, of course.

The teacher wore expensively tailored ivory linen slacks and a matching jersey shirt that dipped low in front, revealing the voluptuous curves of her breasts. Her red hair was a rich coppery shade, worn shoulder-length with a windblown look that was somehow sensual and matched her full-lipped mouth. Leigh felt nerves stabbing in her midriff as tawny, almond-shaped eyes scrutinized her intently.

Rod stood to greet the newcomer. "Hello, Phyllis. You haven't met Doctor Leigh Alexander, have you? She's our new veterinarian. Leigh, this is Phyllis Calhoun."

Phyllis seemed to pose there like a beauty queen about to make a dramatic entrance. She tossed her gleaming hair back in a practiced and seductive gesture before inclining her head to Leigh. "Doctor. So you are Shane's new employee. You will forgive me if I say you aren't exactly what I expected." Her voice had a husky edge to it.

"How do you do, Miss Calhoun." Leigh sensed an instant antagonism in the red-haired woman, a coiled, intense dislike that was all too apparent in the flare of her delicate nostrils. Then Phyllis darted an openly calculating look from Leigh back to Rod.

"I see you are introducing Leigh to our quaint little metropolis, Rod." Her tone indicated she found San Lorenzo hateful, rather than quaint.

"I do my best," said Rod with a mock bow.

Phyllis slid her gaze back to Leigh. "We shall undoubtedly become better acquainted. I am frequently at the ranch with Shane."

"Since I have work to do there, if we see each other at all it will be only in passing."

"Shane is a demanding employer." Phyllis raked a carefully manicured hand slowly through flaming tresses. "Just as he is demanding in other areas."

Leigh knew what she was implying and felt her cheeks grow warm. How easy it was to imagine those strong arms of Shane's gathering that enticing figure close against his hard muscles and warm, tanned skin. How clearly she could see those moist, red lips laughing before being claimed by Shane's ruthless mouth.

Phyllis smiled, and Leigh saw the malice in her eyes a moment before she spoke. "I wish you luck, my dear."

"She doesn't have to depend on luck, Phyllis," said Rod gallantly. "Leigh happens to be extremely competent."

"Is that so?" Phyllis cast a disdainful glance at Leigh.

"Rod exaggerates," Leigh said, giving him a warning look. "The truth is, I feel fortunate to have this job at all."

"That seems a fair assessment," Phyllis returned with an impudent smirk.

Leigh felt a weakness in the pit of her stomach as she realized that this woman was enraged by her presence in Shane's house in whatever capacity.

"Please excuse me," Phyllis said abruptly. "I see my

friend has taken care of our check and is waiting for me."
She swayed across the dining room toward the woman
who stood near the door. Leigh saw Phyllis bend close to
the other woman to whisper something as the two left together.

"I don't think she liked you much," Rod said, sitting
down again.

"She's very pretty," Leigh returned, unwilling to take
the bait.

"In her way," agreed Rod, and the secret smile was
back. It was beginning to irritate Leigh. "Just as you are
beautiful in yours."

She had already seen enough of Rod's deliberate charm
with women to be unimpressed by the compliment. She
finished her coffee. "I think I'd better go back to the ranch
now. Tomorrow will be another hard day."

An impatient expression crossed his face. "Ever the dedicated career woman, aren't you?"

"Why is it," Leigh retorted, "that no one thinks it
strange for a man to be dedicated to his career? But when
it's a woman—well, there must be something wrong with
her!"

Rod was instantly apologetic. "I didn't mean it like
that."

"I am glad you didn't," said Leigh gravely, "or my good
opinion of you would have gone down the tubes."

"So you have formed a good opinion of me." His tone
was bantering. That's a step in the right direction."

During the drive back to the ranch, Rod returned to the
subject of his heifers, as if he feared anything more personal might antagonize Leigh further. As for Leigh, she
relaxed at the change of topic and they were soon parked
in front of the ranch house. Rod helped her out, taking
her arm as they walked toward the house. In the foyer she
turned to him. "Thank you for dinner."

She was not prepared for his swift action and, therefore,
did not manage to turn her face aside in time to avoid his
kiss, which lacked every sensation for Leigh except anger
at being taken by surprise. She managed to get her arms

between them and pushed her hands against his chest until the embrace was broken.

His blue eyes had a glazed look, as if his passion had been fanned to flames by the kiss. How strange that he should feel so much, while her only desire was to get away from him as soon as possible. Yet she did not flatter herself that he found her more desirable than the numbers of other women he had known. She felt sure any one of them could have caused the same reaction. The Casey brothers had Irish blood and, from all she had heard, the Irish were a volatile, passionate people. It was unfortunate that Shane Casey did not share with his brother the charm of the Irish as well.

Rod was looking puzzled. She bit back the angry words that had risen to her lips. It wasn't in her to humiliate him for something as meaningless as a good-night kiss. "Thank you again, Rod, and good night," she said and turned away from him to walk briskly down the hall to her apartment, the sound of her high heels echoing in the silent house.

Saturday morning was clear and languidly beautiful and the birds in the palm trees had been singing their praises to the new day since before dawn. Only the day before, Leigh had discovered that her shuttered kitchen window overlooked a luxurious oval swimming pool situated on one end of a large courtyard and surrounded by palms and exotic flowers in geometrically designed beds. On arising, she went to stand at the window and watch redbirds making graceful dips over the pool and a toad hopping about the soft-pink paving of the pool apron and patio.

Brilliant sunlight and a vivid blue sky—a day made for youth and adventure.

Leigh felt a happy anticipation at the prospect of spending the day with her old friend Bruce Landing. She had called him the day before, and his eagerness to see her again had been salve to an ego bruised by the unflattering reactions she seemed to evoke in her employer and his "friend," Phyllis Calhoun. And even though Rod's response to her was kinder, she had found herself since

Thursday evening going out of her way to avoid meeting him.

So she was looking forward to getting away for the day. First, of course, there was the unpleasant prospect of the drive to San Antonio with Shane. She had seen little of him since their ride together Thursday afternoon. Now she determined not to allow her discomfort with Shane to spoil her day with Bruce.

Turning aside from the idyllic view, she went into her bedroom and dressed in a soft, cool pantsuit of aqua crepe. The pullover top was sleeveless and gathered in soft folds at shoulder and waist. With the pantsuit she wore a narrow gold neck chain and comfortable bone sandals.

She arrived in the foyer at the same time that her employer appeared from the direction of his study, wearing soft gray slacks and a white knit shirt that made his tanned skin look even darker. They left immediately in Shane's gleaming black Mercedes.

"Is your friend expecting you?" he asked as they turned onto the highway.

"Yes. He said he'd meet me in front of the Alamo."

"Then I'll deliver you there and go on to my business meeting. I don't know what time I'll be through, but when I am, I'll get the supplies on the list you gave me."

"I could do that if you think you'll be pressed for time," she offered, glancing at his profile. "Bruce has a car, and I'm sure he wouldn't mind driving me."

"No. I'll do it." His eyes were on the road, but she was uncomfortably aware of his solid bulk in the seat beside her. "You shouldn't have to worry about business today," he said unexpectedly. "Do you know San Antonio well?"

"Not well at all. I only passed through the outskirts on my way to the ranch."

"It has an atmosphere all its own. It's an amalgam of old and new and still very Spanish, not only in its heritage, but in its daily routine."

"It should be interesting." This sounded stilted, even to her own ears.

Shane turned his head for a second to look at her.

"Especially in the company of a young man you seem happy to be meeting."

"Yes, I am looking forward to seeing Bruce," she said without much expression. "He's an old and good friend."

"Your relationship with him is merely friendship then?" he asked, returning his eyes to the road.

Her impression of Thursday afternoon returned, a feeling that he was far more interested in her personal life than his position as her employer warranted. She still suspected he was hoping she would marry and leave the ranch, but she resented this kind of question from him.

"Yes," she replied shortly.

"Perhaps my brother is more to your liking."

"I hope Rod will also be my friend."

"And what of romance?" She could hear the wry amusement in his tone.

"I don't need constant romantic involvement to have a satisfying life," she returned stiffly.

"Really?" A faintly bitter smile touched the hard edge of his mouth. "I know you're a liberated career woman, but you're also human, and I have noticed that women have the same needs as men."

"Most women, maybe."

"But you're different?" He laughed softly. "No, Leigh, and I don't think you believe that either. You must have looked into a mirror lately. Those lips were made for kissing. That body was made to fit into a man's arms."

Her sharp intake of breath was audible. Heat flamed in her cheeks. He must enjoy embarrassing her. She was convinced there was a cruel streak in this man. "I—I do not wish to continue this conversation."

"Whatever you say." The words were polite, but she knew that inside he was laughing at her.

During the remainder of the hour's drive, Shane's conversation could not have been more circumspect. Nevertheless, she could not entirely relax for she still remained fearful of what he might say next.

At last they reached the city and passed through streets of gleaming white bungalows and villas, each with its palm trees and banana plants and enchanting garden, bright with hibiscus and jasmine. The heavy scent of perfume-laden blossoms wafted through the open window of the car.

When the black Mercedes came to a stop on Broadway, near Brackenridge Park, Shane turned to her. "I'll meet you this evening at the Tower of the Americas Restaurant. It's in Hemisfair Plaza atop the tower."

She had opened the car door and started to get out. She turned back to ask, "What time?"

"Eight o'clock, if that suits your schedule. I thought we could have dinner before returning to the ranch. Bring your friend, if you like."

"Eight will be fine." She closed the car door behind her and started toward the Alamo. She saw Bruce hurrying along the boardwalk, smiling.

"Leigh," he exclaimed as they met. "It's great to see you!" He grabbed her in a bear hug, and she responded with a tinkling laugh as he let her go. Smiling up at his ruddy face, she said, "How I've looked forward to today!" Glancing over her shoulder, she saw the black Mercedes still parked at the curb. She took a step toward it questioningly, wondering if Shane wanted to say something else to her before departing. But then the car moved into the traffic and was gone.

Bruce took her on a walking tour of the city. Their first stop, of course, was the Alamo. As Leigh stood in the cool main hall of the ancient mission, she sensed the unseen presence of Crockett and Bowie and the rest of that reckless and valiant crew that made a shambles of a mighty army before it fell under sheer weight of numbers. Though they had been outgunned and outnumbered, the spirit that made those hundred eighty-seven men fight to the death inside the Alamo's walls had caused them to live on as a symbol of courage for future generations, and it was impossible to stand where they had stood without feeling this.

From the Alamo they wandered through the Paseo del Rio, where the walkways were bordered by quaint shops, art galleries, and places to eat. At noon, they stopped for lunch at an outdoor restaurant that featured French cuisine. And after lunch, while the shops were closed for siesta, they boarded a boat for sightseeing on the San Antonio River.

More than two hours later, feeling rested after their boat ride, they decided to walk to the Military Plaza, where they viewed the statue of Moses Austin, and the Governor's Palace with its adobe walls.

It was growing late by the time they reached La Villita and, upon passing through the entryway, entered nineteenth-century Spanish Texas. Leigh was charmed by the quaint village within a city, standing in the very shadow of downtown skyscrapers. As they left La Villita, Leigh sighed loudly, partly in exhaustion and partly in regret that their tour was finished.

"There are a lot of other interesting things we haven't seen yet," Bruce said. "There are four old-world missions in the city in addition to the Alamo. And there's a Buckhorn Hall of Horns you'd get a kick out of."

"Please," Leigh groaned. "I'd love to see everything, but I'm ready to drop."

He glanced at his wristwatch. "Time we headed for the restaurant." A melancholy look crossed his face. "Where has the day gone? It seems as if you couldn't have been here more than an hour or two."

Leigh laughed. "My feet say otherwise."

"You must come back again soon."

"I'd like to," she said sincerely. "Now, that has to be our restaurant over there."

He took her arm and led her across the street to the Hemisfair Plaza, which was dominated by a tall tower.

Gazing upward, Leigh asked, "How far does it go?"

"Seven hundred and fifty feet," he told her. "And the restaurant is at the very top. It revolves every hour for a change in view."

"What fun!" Leigh exclaimed. Her day with Bruce had given her back her cheerfully confident outlook. She felt free and independent again, capable of tackling almost anything. But this feeling dimmed as they stepped off the elevator and met Shane at the entrance to the restaurant.

Leigh made the introductions, and Shane led them to

the table he had already reserved. It was next to the glass and, after being seated, Leigh gazed down at the city where the lights were beginning to come on. "It's so pretty, isn't it?"

The two men agreed, and Shane began to ask Bruce about his work, skillfully drawing him out. For some reason Leigh had not expected him to be as successful in relationships with men as he apparently was with women. To her surprise Bruce liked Shane. Of course, he had heard about Shane's horses, and his admiration for the man was obvious. The meal passed with a feeling of goodwill about the table.

It was with reluctance that Leigh left the restaurant and said good-bye to Bruce outside. The earlier feeling of camaraderie that had seemed a part of the threesome in the restaurant fled as she accompanied Shane to the Mercedes. But she was so tired that her nerves would not take any more jangling, and by the time they had reached the outskirts of the city, she was fast asleep, blissfully unaware that her head had slumped to one side and was resting against Shane's broad shoulder.

The next thing she knew, Shane was shaking her gently. She sat up, confused, her eyes blinking open. "Where are we?"

"In the garage at the ranch."

She looked around her in the dimness, unable to believe she had slept through the entire drive. "I—didn't mean to fall asleep."

He got out of the car and came around to open her door. "Landing must have given you a workout. You were dead to the world."

She stepped out of the car and walked a few steps, pausing on the drive just outside the garage to look up at the blanket of stars in the distant sky. "How lovely it all is," she murmured, hardly aware of the man who had stopped so near her.

"You are in a good mood. Your day must have been enjoyable." She started at the voice so close behind her and, turning, gazed up into his shadowed face. There was enough light from the yard lamps for her to see how his eyes scanned her face, the lashes dark against the planes of his rugged features.

Her eyes met his, she hoped with sufficient assurance to convince him she was calm, not quaking inside at his nearness. "Yes, it's fun to be with good friends."

His eyes roved the sheen of her hair. She was not aware that her eyes, still slightly swollen from sleep, had a seductive look and that this impression was heightened by the tousled, tumbling half-waves against her cheek.

"Landing wants much more from you than friendship," he murmured.

She regarded him with scorn. "I suppose you think it's impossible for a man and a woman to have a close relationship without sex."

"Not impossible, but highly unlikely." His tone mocked her.

"I think—" She stammered, a strange, boneless feeling creeping over her, frightening her. It was as if something primitive in her gave in to his overwhelmingly male strength, even while she resented and despised him. "I think your attitude is disgusting!"

"But realistic," he said with quiet intensity. His dark brows drew together, adding harshness to the hard bone-structure of his face. "Landing's dearest wish is to get you in bed. It's obvious every time he looks at you."

She refused to believe him. She would not allow him to spoil a fine and innocent relationship with his cynical outlook. "Why must you degrade every man to your own filthy level?" she said between teeth that chattered slightly.

Hands gripped her shoulders—hard, warm, pulling her relentlessly toward him. "Don't talk like a foolish child! You may be inexperienced, but you are a woman with a woman's emotions."

She was deeply shocked by her body's response. Every cell and nerve quivered expectantly at his cruel touch. He stared down at her, his face lean, the cheeks slashed by dark shadows, and her heart beat thunderously in her ears as the silence hung between them.

"And since I am a mere woman, I surely cannot resist the great Shane Casey!" she flung at him. She gave a furious jerk to free herself of his grasp. But he was too quick for her, and she was gripped even harder and yanked against him, her cry of protest crushed by his lips as he kissed her with bruising force. The entire length of her body was aware of the hard muscle and bone pressing against it. She fought to free herself, but it was like fighting a solid wall.

She felt so very weak, unable to struggle any more, and she gave up trying to keep her lips clamped together against the merciless assault. As her lips opened, his kiss became gentler, his tongue probing slowly in her unresistant mouth, drawing a moan from her.

Leigh had never been kissed like this . . . never experienced anything so mindlessly dreamlike . . . never known a sensation that was half ecstasy and half torture. She had been furious enough to claw his eyes out and now, she realized with a shock, her fingers caressed the nape of his neck. It was madness!

She tore free of him, panting. "Don't ever touch me again!"

"Then don't ask for it," he said deliberately.

Leigh's fingers curled into fists, yet she still recognized an impulse somewhere within her pounding heart to touch him again . . . Oh, it was humiliating!

His eyes swept over her. "My point is well-taken. You are a normal, healthy woman like every other woman."

"And you," she said tiredly, "are an egotistical devil." She pushed dispiritedly at her heavy hair, feeling bruised and utterly exhausted. She walked away from him, her head held high with an effort. There was a tremor in her hand as she let herself in the front door.

High heels clicked across the tile toward her. She looked up and was face to face with Phyllis Calhoun.

"Where is Shane?" Her voice was silky with menace.

Leigh was spared the necessity of answering when Shane stepped into the foyer and Phyllis's furious, tawny eyes flicked from Leigh to the tall man behind her.

"Where have you been?"

"I'm sure you have talked to Maggie and know we've

been in San Antonio." There was a warning in the low voice. "You shouldn't have waited."

"You've forgotten, haven't you? We had a date tonight. I cooked dinner for you at my place hours ago."

He ran a hand through dark hair. "Phyllis, I'm sorry. I did forget."

The redhead's back went rigid and her long fingernails curled against her palms. Then her gaze scraped Leigh's tousled hair and she said shrilly, "I won't be treated like this! How dare you stand me up and go out with this— this common—"

"Be quiet, Phyllis!" Shane ordered. "We'll talk about this later."

Phyllis stood, as if poised for attack, staring at him, her nostrils flaring. Leigh took the opportunity to leave them alone.

As she made her way down the hall she heard Phyllis's voice dripping with venom. "I see you have wasted no time in adding your *veterinarian* to your string of conquests! Really, Shane, I thought you had more class!"

It was obvious that Shane was straining for control as he returned coldly, "I'll take you home, Phyllis. And I do not intend to discuss this any further."

When Leigh reached her apartment she locked herself in and, without turning on the lights, dropped, fully clothed, upon the bed.

FIVE

Leigh's heart continued to thud dully as she lay across her bed. She rolled onto her back, staring through her bedroom window at the stars in the clear night sky. She heard the Mercedes' motor roar to life in the garage, which was not far from her window, and then the car backing over gravel and turning; finally the sound dimmed and disappeared as Shane and Phyllis left the house and headed for San Lorenzo. She wondered fleetingly how Phyllis had arrived at the ranch. There had been no extra car parked in front or in the garage area. Obviously she had asked a friend to drive her, thereby forcing Shane to take her home. As Rod had said, Phyllis Calhoun was the sort of woman who was relentless when it came to getting what she wanted. She would make a formidable enemy.

Leigh shrank inwardly as she saw again the pure hatred in Phyllis's eyes as they had rested on her in the foyer. She had, from time to time, had to fight male prejudice in her chosen profession, but never had she come up against such hostility in a woman.

Leigh drew a long, shuddering breath, the sound somehow deeply melancholy in the silence of the apartment. Shane would be able to coax Phyllis into a better mood. Clearly he'd had much experience in handling women. Her imagination pictured Shane and Phyllis alone in the redhead's living quarters; she had a swift mental picture of her employer dissipating Phyllis's fury—and doing it with practiced ease. It would pose no problem at all for Shane to go from kissing Leigh with such harsh cruelty to making love to Phyllis.

She made a cynical sound as she remembered Rod's warning: *Shane is a man who enjoys variety in his women*. Leigh did not delude herself for one moment that Shane Casey's feelings when he had kissed her were anything more than purely physical. He was not accustomed to having a woman resist his advances. Consequently she might represent something of a challenge to his oversize male ego, but certainly nothing more.

What disturbed her more than anything, however, was her own shocking reaction. What had come over her? She had felt, for a moment, totally incapable of controlling her own actions.

Unable to lie still, she got up and paced the dark bedroom in a fresh flash of annoyance. How dare he grab her like some giggling hired girl! How dare he even touch her—let alone kiss her with such bruising force that she had briefly lost contact with reality! But only briefly! She had not been able to think clearly enough at the time to tell him what she really thought of him. Oh, now, she could think of several fitting epithets! He was the most arrogant, conniving, ruthless man she'd ever encountered. He would resort to any underhanded trick to have his own way. He obviously believed that, should he choose to do more than kiss her, she would not be able to resist!

Leigh had wandered into the kitchen and, as this thought struck her, she came to a halt, gripping the back of one of the kitchen chairs. Was there some truth in such an assumption? For one moment there, while he was kissing her . . .

You are a normal healthy woman, like every other woman, he had said. Those words told her exactly what he thought of her. She was only a woman, like all the others, one in a long succession who had succumbed to Shane Casey's charms. For, as she had learned tonight, he could turn on charm, of a crude sort, when it suited his purpose. Perhaps he believed, too, that her situation as his employee put her at a disadvantage. Well, forewarned was forearmed. What happened with Shane tonight must never be allowed to happen again.

This determination hardened as the minutes passed. She left off pacing and took a long shower before going back to bed and, this time, to sleep.

*   *   *

The next morning was as clear and bright as the previous day, filled with the songs of the birds who lived in the trees that surrounded the poolside patio. Leigh awoke rested, her confidence restored, eager to be about her work, certain that nothing could occur that she could not handle deftly. It was almost as if that disturbing moment of time with Shane on the graveled drive had never happened.

After breakfast, eaten at the small table while looking out upon the lovely courtyard beyond her window, Leigh remembered, with a slight jolt, that it was Sunday, another day off. Thinking of the long hours of idleness that stretched before her, she decided to take Skipper for a ride about the ranch. Maggie was having a cup of coffee at the kitchen table when Leigh passed through.

"You're up early," the housekeeper greeted her.

"Not really. It's after eight."

Maggie twisted to look at the kitchen wall clock. "Well, it is, sure enough. I didn't realize because Mr. Shane is usually up by this time." She frowned slightly. "It seems both he and Mr. Rod are sleeping in today. Were you late getting back from San Antonio?"

Leigh shook her head, thinking that it wasn't *she* who had kept Shane out late. In fact, she wondered if he'd come home at all. She left Maggie and headed for the barn, but curiosity impelled her to glance toward the garages as she passed to see if Shane's car was back. It was.

José was cleaning out one of the horse stalls when she arrived at the barn. "Good morning," she greeted him cheerily. "How's Lady today?"

José's grin split his brown face. "Much better, Doctor Leigh. She doesn't limp much at all now."

"It might be wise to give her another antibiotic injection," Leigh said. She prepared the antibiotic and José accompanied her to the outside corral where Lady was penned. The mare took little notice of Leigh this morning and suffered the injection with hardly a flinch. Leigh ran a hand along the mare's neck, her touch detecting no fever. Lady was definitely on the mend.

José had made a pot of coffee on the hot plate and insisted that she join him in a cup. They were seated on bales of hay at one end of the barn when Manuel appeared.

His brown eyes lighted up when he saw Leigh. "I can help you today if you need me," he announced. "I looked for you yesterday, but Mr. Rod said you weren't here."

Remembering the boxes of medicines and supplies still in the back seat of the Mercedes, Leigh said, "As it happens, *amigo*, you *can* help me. I need to put away some things in the cabinets here. Let me finish my coffee, and we'll get started."

José insistèd on accompanying them back to the car, and he carried the largest box as they returned to the barn. "You see, I've arranged things alphabetically," Leigh told Manuel when José had gone back to cleaning stalls. "You know your ABC's, don't you? See if you can help me line everything up on the cabinet first."

Manuel set to work with a vengeance, his small brow furrowing as he deciphered the first letter of the incomprehensible terms on the medicine boxes. He tried, without much success, to sound out the name on one box. "I have never heard of such words," he said, baffled. "English has many words to learn."

Leigh laughed. "No more than Spanish has, I'm sure. But you don't have to be able to read these words. Just so you can tell what the first letters are."

"Oh, I can do that," Manuel assured her proudly. "I was the first one in my first-grade class to learn the English letters." His small, mischievous face clouded. "My first-grade teacher liked me. She told me I was smart." He looked wistful. "But she might have been wrong."

"Of course she wasn't wrong," Leigh protested. "You *are* a bright boy, Manuel."

His pink tongue protruded, caught between his teeth, as he concentrated on the boxes. Leigh thought he hadn't heard her, but after a few moments, he mused, "Miss Calhoun says I am"—he seemed to search his mind for the word—"slow. Slow to learn, she says." He looked up at Leigh gravely. "I may have to go into the special class next year."

With an effort Leigh bit back a bitter criticism of Manuel's teacher. The energetic, eager child beside her was no more retarded than Leigh was! Surely the school board would not allow this injustice to be done to Manuel. But Shane was on the school board, and Leigh did not know how much influence Phyllis Calhoun had on him when she chose to exercise it. Leigh was inclined to think it might be a considerable amount.

"Tell me, Manuel," Leigh said a little later, "when you talk with your parents at home, do you use Spanish?"

"*Sí*," the boy said. "Mama says it is easier. We can talk much faster in Spanish."

A good while later, after Manuel had helped Leigh place all the supplies on the cabinet top, she thanked him and told him she'd put the boxes on the shelves. He beamed at her and said he was going back home to see if Paco, the family dog, had had her puppies yet. He darted out of the barn and José, who had just finished cleaning the stalls, lounged against the cabinet while Leigh finished the job of putting the supplies away.

"It will be at least three weeks yet before that dog has pups," he said with an indulgent smile. "But Manuel keeps a close watch on her."

"He's a delightful boy," Leigh said.

José nodded, clearly pleased with the compliment. "He is a good worker. He will make a good ranch hand some day."

"If that's what he wants," Leigh ventured hesitantly. "But Manuel may decide to leave the ranch when he's older." She stopped working to look at the boy's father steadily. "From what I've seen, he's intelligent enough to be whatever he wants to be."

José frowned sadly. "This I used to think, also. I used to talk to Manuel about finishing school, maybe going away to—what do you call it?—ah, yes, university. But now—" One hand turned out in a gesture of futility.

"I don't see why Manuel couldn't go to a university if he wanted. If it's money that concerns you, there are always scholarships."

"No." José's expression was one of regret. "Mr. Shane would help us with the money. But a boy must be very smart—" He touched his forehead with a brown finger. "Very intelligent to go to university."

"Manuel *is* intelligent."

"No. He falls behind his class. He cannot read as he should. His teacher tells us he is—" He shrugged helplessly. "I cannot think of the words she used, but she meant that Manuel could not learn as he should. His learning is . . . crippled."

"Disabled?" Leigh supplied.

"Yes, that is the word. Manuel is disabled in his learning. Those were her words."

"I don't believe it!" Leigh could not stop herself. "You cannot accept this, José. Miss Calhoun is not infallible. She can be wrong."

José's shrug was philosophical. "She is a teacher. Teachers know about such things." Leigh was deeply disturbed at the Mexican man's seeming willingness to believe Manuel was retarded on the say-so of one woman. Leigh was convinced there was something else—some personal grudge against the child or his family—that was behind Phyllis's determination to remove Manuel from her class.

Not trusting herself to discuss Phyllis Calhoun any longer, Leigh said, "I think I'll take Skipper for a ride when I've finished here."

"I'll saddle him for you."

"Oh, that isn't necessary, José. I'm sure you have other things to do. I can saddle my own horse."

"No," he said stubbornly. "Mr. Shane would not like it. I am to help you. He would be very angry with me if I permitted you to saddle your own horse."

"Well, we can't allow Mr. Shane to become angry, can we?"

Missing the sarcasm in her tone, José smiled and nodded, leaving her to go saddle Skipper. As she finished putting the supplies on the shelves, Leigh pondered what José had said about Manuel's difficulty with reading. It was entirely possible that the problem was due to the fact that the Gomezes spoke Spanish at home. Manuel may not be familiar enough with the English words to translate the printed form into speech quickly. Whatever the problem, however, Leigh was certain it had nothing to do with Manuel's intelligence. It could be that he only needed special help with reading. But wouldn't Phyllis have detected that? It would seem to be the first thing that would oc-cur to a teacher when dealing with a child from a non-English-speaking home.

A few minutes later she rode away from the barn on the chestnut gelding. It was a pleasant day for riding, and she spent more than two hours on horseback. Finally she stopped to watch some of the ranch's finest horses as they grazed near a small pond. What beautiful animals they were! All of them appeared to be in good health, and she intended to keep them that way. The matter of their inoc-ulation and treatment schedules seemed of paramount im-portance. She decided to tackle whatever records Doctor Smith had left behind first thing Monday morning.

It was after two when she returned to the house. Maggie intercepted her in the hallway, her hazel eyes raking over Leigh's rumpled jeans and damp shirt with seeming disap-proval. "You come on in the kitchen and let me fix you a fruit salad or something," she ordered, her tone brooking no refusal. "There's no earthly reason for you to work seven days a week and fix your own meals to boot."

Leigh laughed and followed the tall housekeeper into the kitchen willingly. "A fruit salad sounds wonderful, Maggie. But I haven't been working much. I took one of the horses for a ride." She sank into a kitchen chair while Maggie went to the refrigerator.

"Mr. Rod's out at the pool," Maggie said as she ar-ranged pieces of fruit on lettuce leaves. "He said for you to come on out."

"I'm not sure I'd feel right about using the pool," Leigh said.

Maggie turned a surprised look on her. "Oh, pshaw! Why, Mr. Shane won't care, if that's what's bothering you." She sniffed. "I must say you're mighty concerned about imposing around here. Why, Doctor Smith didn't let that bother him. He acted just like one of the family." She poured a glass of iced tea and carried it, along with the fruit salad, to Leigh.

"Oh, how delicious-looking!" Leigh exclaimed.

"You needn't be changing the subject, either," Maggie said. "You just go on out to the pool when you're finished eating."

Leigh lifted a cold, sweet chunk of fresh pineapple to her mouth. "Where is Shane?"

"In the study, I think," Maggie told her as she ran water into the sink. "He's as much of a workhorse as you are, only I'm used to him."

Leigh smiled and finished the fruit salad, thinking that, since Shane was occupied elsewhere, she might join Rod at the pool after all. A few minutes later she left her apartment, wearing a lime-green bikini with a towel draped over her shoulders, and let herself out a door which opened on the back courtyard. She walked across the pale pink patio, stepping quickly because the pavement was a little too warm for comfort. Nearer the pool, forest-green turf absorbed some of the heat.

Rod, who was sitting on the edge of the pool at the shallow end, drinking a soft drink from a can, gave an appreciative whistle. "I was about to give up on you. Where have you been?"

Leigh stepped onto the diving board. "Horseback riding." She walked to the end of the board and dived in. When she came up, she swam to where Rod was sitting and caught hold of the pool's overhanging edge.

Looking down at her, Rod's blue eyes narrowed as they swept over her bare shoulders and the curve of her breasts above the bikini top. "I haven't seen much of you since our dinner together the other night. You're not avoiding me, are you?"

"Don't be silly. I've been busy."

"With big brother," Rod drawled a little childishly.

Leigh raked her wet hair away from her face and smiled at him, determined to ignore his sullen mood. "He *is* my employer, Rod."

Rod made a sound of disgust. "I'm not likely to forget that, am I? You won't let me."

She changed the subject blithely. "How are your heifers doing?"

"Fine," he replied shortly. He gestured toward an ice chest sitting a few feet away. "How about a cold drink?"

"Let me swim the length of the pool a few times, and then I'll have a cola, thank you." A while later she climbed out, retrieved her towel, and dropped onto a pool

lounge near Rod, rubbing her arms and legs dry and tow-
eling her blond hair briskly.

Sighing with pleasant tiredness, she stretched full-length
on the lounge as Rod handed her a chilled cola can.
"Ummm," Leigh murmured after a long swallow. "That
hits the spot. It can get hot in Texas."

Rod pulled his lounge closer to hers and lay down.
"Like an oven sometimes. There's a story told about one
of the trail hands who helped drive a herd of longhorns up
the Chisholm trail one summer. When he got to Kansas,
somebody asked him how he liked Texas. He replied that
if he owned Hell and Texas, he'd rent out Texas and live
in Hell."

Leigh laughed. "Well, no place is perfect. But a little
hot weather is a small price to pay for living here, isn't
it?"

Rod shot her a reproachful look. "You sound like
Shane. The land! Good Lord, the land is everything, every
precious inch of it. Even the parts that are good for nothing—except maybe to hold the world together." He
laughed, but without humor.

Leigh felt a stab of sympathy for the man beside her,
who seemed so unhappy with his lot. "Do you still want to
sell your half of the ranch?"

"I'd put it on the market tomorrow, if Shane would
agree." There was vehemence in his tone. "Not that he
ever will! He and my father were cut out of the same
mold—stubborn as mules. My father thought he knew
what was best for everybody else, and so does Shane."

"You don't enjoy ranching, do you?"

He made a sound of disgust. "I'm not cut out for the
grueling hard work which, as often as not, results in little
or no profit."

Leigh had not noticed that Rod worked *that* hard. Certainly he didn't put in the long hours his brother did. She
might have made a joke about this, but Rod was deadly
serious.

"There are much easier eays to make a living," Rod
went on.

"But your brother seems to have done very well."

"Oh, Shane—" There was thick resentment in the words. "He's not like other men, or haven't you noticed?"

Yes, she had noticed, Leigh thought uncomfortably, but not the way Rod meant.

"In fact," Rod was saying, "I sometimes wonder if he's human." He turned his face away from her, a dark frown creasing the clean-cut lines.

Leigh closed her eyes, feeling the sun warm on her body, and thinking that Shane's refusal to allow Rod to sell his land was just another example of her employer's ruthlessly indomitable will. But this clash of purposes, which Rod seemed incapable of winning, was no concern of hers; nor was she in any position to take sides. She was almost asleep when she became aware that someone was standing over her. Her eyes flew open and she saw Shane, in dark blue swimming trunks, looking down at her with an unreadable expression on his rugged, tanned face.

Leigh sat up. "Why didn't you say something? It's frightening being crept up on."

Shane grinned and, spreading his towel on the turf, sat down beside her. "Sorry." But the twinkle in his eyes denied the word. On her other side Rod stirred, greeted his brother perfunctorily, closed his eyes, and turned away from them as if to sleep. Leigh, however, suspected he simply wanted to avoid conversation with his brother.

"Maggie said you went riding this morning," Shane commented, looking at Leigh from beneath thick, dark lashes. He sat with legs drawn up, long muscular arms wound loosely around his knees. His chest and legs were as tanned as his arms, she noticed. Black hair curled on his chest and trailed in a narrow line out of sight below the waistband of his trunks. Leigh was suddenly too aware of the solid masculinity of the man who sat with one bare broad shoulder almost touching her leg.

"I did," she said, "after I put away the supplies."

He slanted a disapproving look at her. "We don't ordinarily work on Sundays," he drawled. "There's such a thing as being too conscientious."

"So I've been told," she retorted, stung by his condescending tone. "Apparently the Sundays-off rule doesn't

74

apply to you either. Maggie said you were working in the study."

He shrugged. "The boss always works harder than anybody." His gray gaze was traveling up her slender legs, across her bare midriff, and now lingered on her breasts. She felt abruptly much too exposed in the scanty bikini. "On my ride," she said quickly, seeking to divert his attention, "I noticed a roan mare who looks ready to drop a foal soon. Isn't it a little late in the year?"

He pulled his gaze from her body and settled it on her face. "She's due in a couple of weeks. Actually I hadn't intended to breed her at all this year. She had a lingering respiratory ailment last spring and summer. She wasn't in any condition to be bred during the regular breeding season. Unfortunately one of my best stallions broke through the fence and got into the corral with her." His eyes held hers, a teasing gleam in the gray depths. "It's practically impossible to thwart a determined male."

Leigh forced herself to meet his gaze. "When the female is trapped in a pen with no way of escape."

He chuckled wickedly and got to his feet. "Race you the length of the pool," he challenged.

She picked up her towel and pulled it around her shoulders. "I've had enough for today," she said pointedly, still warm with embarrassment at his suggestive banter about the horses.

"You're not one for taking chances, are you, Leigh?" Shane called after her as she walked away.

She turned to glare at him. "Only when I think the stakes are worth it," she shot back and then, turning again, she hurried toward the house, hearing Shane's laughter before he dived into the pool.

Back in her apartment, she struggled for a moment in a haze of indignation and dismay about the wisdom of remaining in Shane Casey's house. It was still possible to go to him and say their arrangement was not working out as she had hoped and ask to be released from their agreement. But in the light of the exchange at the pool just now, he would most certainly interpret this as self-doubt on her part. He would say—with that maddening sneer—that he had known she couldn't handle the job all along.

Hadn't he tried to warn her? Did she really want to give him that satisfaction?

And what would become of Manuel if she left? Who would take his side against the formidable Phyllis Calhoun? Not that Leigh had any clear idea yet how she might go about this. But somehow she must try to help Manuel, for she seemed to be the only one who did not believe the teacher's assessment of his capabilities. So, as tempting as it might be to pack up and leave her job, determination to stand up to Shane Casey and compassion for the boy Manuel took over. She had to stay, she acknowledged, and felt the tightening in the pit of her stomach.

She kept to her apartment for the rest of the day. She wrote a long letter to Jess Harlan, describing the ranch, the horses, what she had accomplished during her first days on the job. Then she wrote of the day spent in San Antonio with Bruce Landing, a favorite of her guardian's, but she carefully avoided anything but the merest mention of the Casey brothers.

About nine that evening there was a knock at Leigh's door. She opened it to find Rod Casey standing in the hall, holding two glasses of wine.

"I thought you might like a nightcap." His mood of the afternoon seemed to have been replaced by his more usual stance of geniality.

Leigh, her letter writing finished, had been feeling a little restless. "This is thoughtful of you, Rod. Come in." She accepted one of the glasses and led the way into the living room. She took one of the facing thick-cushioned, Spanish-style chairs, and Rod took the other.

"I wanted to apologize for my black mood earlier," he said as soon as they were seated.

Leigh raised her eyebrows. "It wasn't directed to me."

Rod laughed. "I'm afraid I'm poor company when I'm feeling sorry for myself. It doesn't happen very often, though."

"I'm glad," Leigh said. "I mean, from what you've said, you haven't much choice except to make the best of things as they are."

"I know. It's what my mother did. She died when Shane

was only ten and I, barely six. I don't remember a lot about her, except that she was small and fragile-looking. And I didn't get to spend as much time with her as I would have liked. She worked alongside my father to make the ranch a going concern. In addition to keeping house and caring for Shane and me, she helped with the heavy ranch work—branding, vaccinating cattle, repairing fences—wherever an extra pair of hands was needed."

"How did she die?"

"She came down with a severe case of pneumonia one spring and, although she eventually got out of bed and went about her work, she never completely threw off the effects. She wouldn't listen to my father or the doctor when they tried to send her back to bed. There was too much work to be done on the ranch." He smiled sadly. "She was the only person in the world, except for Shane, that my father couldn't dominate. She died that same year in late summer."

"I'm sorry." Somehow Leigh wished she had better words to offer.

Rod drained his wineglass. "Texas is full of such stories. The people who carved out the state's big ranches didn't do it by working forty-hour weeks."

"I'm sure they took pride in leaving a legacy for their children."

"Yes," Rod said ruefully. "Only sometimes the children don't appreciate it. Isn't that what you're thinking?"

"No," she denied. "Where is it written you have to love ranching because your parents did?"

Rod was looking at her interestedly. "I'm beginning to believe you understand how I feel. It—it might be possible for you to help me."

Leigh shook her head doubtfully. "How?"

"Reason with Shane. He won't listen to me."

Leigh's violet eyes widened with surprise. "What makes you think he'd listen to *me*?"

Rod studied her reflectively. "You're not afraid to stand up to him. I get the feeling he respects you."

Respect! Leigh thought with amazement. It was hardly the word she would have used. "I'm afraid you've come to the wrong place for help in swaying your brother. I'm the last person he'd listen to. You might do better to solicit Phyllis Calhoun's aid."

Rod's expression was sardonic. "Phyllis won't do anything to oppose Shane." He gave an elaborate shrug. "Oh, well, I just thought I'd mention it—in case the opportunity ever comes up."

Leigh had a fleeting impression that Rod had come to the apartment, not to bring her a nightcap, but to approach the subject of her acting as his intermediary with Shane. "I don't think it will," she said truthfully.

Monday morning, in the paneled barn office, Leigh found Doctor Smith's records to be in as big a muddle as the supply cabinet had been. The bottom drawer of the metal desk was crammed with scraps of paper on which horses' names, birth dates, abbreviated descriptions of medications and treatments, or pasture numbers had been scrawled. There was no apparent order to these, and Leigh resigned herself to several days of sorting and trying to deciper the cryptic notes.

She began to place the papers on top of the desk in piles, according to pasture numbers—or individual horses when these were given. In too many cases, a medication was noted or a date given without reference to which horse had received the treatment. Often there was a number in the corner of such a note, and Leigh guessed these must refer to particular horses. If so, there must be a key to the code somewhere; surely she would run across it in due time.

She was soon deeply engrossed in creating a semblance of order from Doctor Smith's chaos. So intense was her absorption that she lost track of the passage of time.

She was made aware of it, however, when Shane Casey barged into the office, carrying a Thermos and a foil-wrapped package.

"Don't you believe in stopping for lunch?" he barked querulously.

Leigh sat back in the creaking swivel chair and stretched her aching back, which had been bent over the desk too long. "I didn't realize it was that late."

"It's almost two." Shane shoved aside a pile of papers

and set the Thermos and the foil package on the littered desktop. "Iced tea and a roast beef sandwich," he said. "Compliments of Maggie who, incidentally, is going to lecture you the next time you show your face at the house. She's already told me off. She thinks I'm a slave driver, and you're not exactly bright to let me get away with it. I'd appreciate it if you'd tell her the overly zealous dedication to your job is your idea, not mine."

Leigh poured tea from the Thermos into its plastic cap and unwrapped the sandwich. "Somehow I doubt that you need anyone to champion your cause."

"I wonder how you mean that," he said dryly.

She lifted her shoulders in a noncommittal gesture and bit into the sandwich, discovering she was famished. The sandwich disappeared speedily along with most of the iced tea. Then she got to her feet, brushed crumbs from her jeans and stood, hands on hips, eyeing the jumbled records on the desk.

Shane had pushed aside another pile of papers and was perched on one corner of the desk. "Can you make heads or tails of this?"

"Some of it. On the other hand—" She took a wrinkled scrap of paper from one pile and showed it to him. "Take this, for example. I have no idea what this number in the corner refers to. There's a whole pile like that. I thought, at first, the numbers must identify particular horses, but so far I haven't found a key with names and numbers."

Shane took the scrap of paper from her hand and scrutinized it. "I think I saw such a key in here some time back." He got up, went around to the front of the desk, and opened another drawer, riffling through more papers. I'm afraid I let these records get out of hand before I realized how carelessly Smith was keeping them."

"Well, I think I can decipher most of this with the key you mentioned and several days of work."

"*Voilà!*" he said triumphantly, pulling a manila folder from the shambles in the drawer. "Here it is." He opened the folder and scanned the contents. "The horses with the red check-marks beside the names aren't here. They're with my trainer near Fort Worth. Two of them are good

79

bets to qualify for the All American Futurity in September."

Having heard for years of the "richest horse race in the world," which was run every year at Ruidoso Downs in New Mexico, Leigh was impressed. She accepted the folder. "This should make the job much easier."

"I'm going to ride over to the old home-place," Shane went on, "and I thought you might like to come along."

"Unless you think you'll need the services of a vet," she demurred, "I'd prefer staying and trying to make some headway here."

His gray eyes were sardonic. "I don't think I'll need a vet. It's just that someone has to check on Rod's heifers and their calves occasionally." His mouth thinned with irritation. "I'm afraid my brother has a rather laissez-faire attitude toward his responsibilities."

Remembering Rod's attendance at the heifers' deliveries and her conversation with him the previous day, Leigh's sympathies were with the younger brother. "He doesn't want to be a rancher, you know."

He gave a short mirthless laugh. "I'd be interested to hear what Rod *does* want to do—in the line of work, I mean. So Rod's been crying on your shoulder, has he? Telling you what a heartless heel I am, I suppose."

"He wouldn't be that unkind," she said angrily. "He just feels frustrated by your refusal to agree to his selling his land. I must admit," she added with a sudden burst of courage, "I understand how he feels. After all, he's a grown man. Surely he can be allowed to make his own decisions." She hadn't intended to get into this with Shane. But somehow the words had come out, against her better judgment. Now Shane was eyeing her with that cold condescension that so infuriated her.

"Hasn't it occurred to you, Leigh," he retorted disdainfully, "that our father must have had good reasons to leave the land to us as he did? He knew that Rod couldn't be counted on to act responsibly."

"From what I've seen of Rod," she said with a toss of her blond hair, "both you and your father have been grossly unfair to him." She knew that she was interfering in family matters that were of no legitimate concern to her. But something in Shane's manner prodded her on. "How can he act responsibly if he's never given the chance?"

Unhurried, Shane felt in his shirt pocket and produced a slim cheroot. He extracted a lighter from another pocket and lighted the cigar, inhaling as he studied her with maddening amusement. While you don't think *I* need a champion, apparently you feel my brother does."

Leigh bit her lip. "I—perhaps I've spoken out of turn. . . ."

The gray eyes narrowed as the smoke from his cheroot filtered upward. "Perhaps you have. Especially since you haven't the slightest notion of what you're talking about. I would advise you to go more slowly in making judgments about people—especially Rod. He can present an abused and righteous facade when it suits him. You might do well to look below the facade before taking up the gauntlet for him so eagerly."

"You're a hard and unfeeling man!" Leigh's eyes blazed. He was so utterly self-assured, and there seemed absolutely nothing she could say that would shake him.

"When I need to be, yes," he replied indolently.

"Well, I'm certainly glad you're not *my* brother!"

"In that, Leigh," he retorted, "we agree." He took another drag on the cheroot. "Since you seem to prefer it, I will leave you with your records. Unless there is something more you would like to discuss." The last was said with a challenging quirk of his finely sculptured mouth. "Any other insults you would like to toss my way before I go?"

"No," she said, determined to remain calm, "not insults, but there is a favor I'd like to ask."

"If this is more to do with Rod—"

"It isn't," she cut in. "It's about Manuel."

The dark brows lifted in surprise. "Oh? I wasn't aware that you knew the boy."

"I do, though," she added, charging ahead, "and I think he's absolutely delightful."

He shrugged disinterestedly. "Do you expect me to disagree with that?"

"It wouldn't surprise me. You're standing by doing nothing while his *teacher*—she emphasized the word sarcastically—"labels him retarded and tries to ruin his entire life!"

He stubbed the cheroot out in an ashtray that sat on the corner of the desk, and looked at her coldly. "I'm curious to know where you came by this information."

"It's not exactly a secret. I know that Phyllis Calhoun wants to have Manuel transferred to a learning-disabled class next year. I also know you're a member of the school board that will make the final decision on Manuel's future."

"It's true that Manuel will be discussed at the next board meeting in July." His head was tilted to one side as he studied her curiously. "But I'm puzzled as to why you're so worked up over this. The Gomezes are virtual strangers to you."

"I can have compassion, even for strangers," she returned, "when I see a flagrant injustice being done."

"Again," he said with calm scrutiny, "I think you're barging into something you don't understand. Since you seem to have discussed this with somebody, you must know that Manuel has been tested repeatedly. Are you suggesting that you are a better judge of the boy's capabilities than tests compiled by experts?"

Leigh felt angry tears pricking her eyelids suddenly, and she brushed them aside with a careless hand. Was she, after all, allowing her liking for the mischievous Manuel to cloud her thinking? She only knew that Shane aroused in her an impotent kind of fury. He was so arrogant and assured. A land baron, a virtual emperor in his own domain. It was positively medieval! It might be childish pique, but she couldn't stand his cold mockery.

"I am suggesting," she said through clenched teeth, "that test results can be rigged. I am suggesting that Phyllis Calhoun, for reasons of her own, has launched a vendetta against a helpless little boy."

He half smiled. "You have certainly taken a dislike to poor Phyllis."

"Oh, I don't expect you to take my word against hers. After all, I'm not your——"

"Yes?" His tone was deceptively soft.

"What I meant to say," she went on in a rush, "was that

my concern here is solely with Manuel. I believe the problem he's had with reading is nothing more than a language barrier caused by the fact that he comes from a Spanish-speaking home. I want to try to help him with his reading."

"So," he said with taunting eyes, "you are a teacher too?"

She folded her fingers into fists, holding them tightly at her sides. "I'll need books—schoolbooks at the third-grade level."

"Ah. . . ." His eyes glinted now. "You want me to get the books for you. Well, it seems to me you have enough to do already." He gestured toward the paper-piled desk.

"I could work with Manuel in the evenings."

He capitulated suddenly. "I'll get the books."

His abrupt change in manner startled her. "Thank you," she said hesitantly.

He slouched on the desk now. "I'm still curious, though," he went on, "as to what is behind your dislike of Phyllis. I could almost believe you're jealous, although why that should be, I can't guess. As you are so fond of reminding me, our relationship—yours and mine—can be only professional."

All at once Leigh felt his male magnetism like a living thing in the small, paneled office and, shivering, she turned to straighten a stack of papers on the desk.

"You aren't jealous of Phyllis, are you, Leigh?" he inquired lazily, getting to his feet as he gazed at her with quiet amusement.

"No, of course not! You are imagining things."

"Oh, I would say you are the one with the oversize imagination here." He paused reflectively. "Interesting to speculate on, nevertheless."

Leigh did not reply. He was only trying to irritate her and she wasn't going to give in to his taunts this time. At least this is what she told herself. But when he continued to watch her silently, she felt her cheeks growing warm, and turned to him, unnerved. "That remark is so typical! You are suggesting that I have some . . . interest in you, apart from my job. Good Lord, what an egotist you are! You think the whole world revolves around you, don't you? Just—please—get out of here and leave me alone!"

From the corner of her eye she saw him move toward her. "Does my presence disturb you, Leigh?"

Leigh swung around to face him, having to look up sharply for he was very near her. "You don't disturb me in the least."

"No?"

"No. Except that I cannot understand your seeming need to run other people's lives."

Shane's gray eyes were suddenly dark and steely with anger. Seeing this, Leigh felt a curious mixture of fear and excitement. Without warning, he gripped her arms and pulled her against him, staring down at her with a smoldering emotion in his eyes that Leigh could not identify. Rage? Hatred? Desire? She had no idea. But every inch of her body was aware of the rock-hard line of him pressing against her, and she could not pull her gaze away from the intensity of those gray eyes.

"Don't," she got out breathlessly. "I told you before, I don't want you to touch me." Her cheeks flamed.

He continued to stare into her eyes as if he were trying, somehow, to penetrate her brain. "You protest too much, Leigh. You *want* me to touch you. You want me to do much more than that."

Leigh shivered and said shakily, "Let me go."

He did so abruptly, and she staggered, supporting herself against the edge of the desk behind her. They stared at each other for another long moment. Then Shane strode toward the door. "You won't always fight me, Leigh," he threw over his shoulder as he left the office, "for the simple reason that you don't want to."

Her indrawn breath was swift. She stared at the closed door and then she buried her face in her hands, wondering in frightened confusion what was happening to her.

SIX

"I'm mighty glad you decided to have dinner with us, Doctor Alexander. Oh, heck, I'll just call you Leigh, if you don't mind." Rex Hemphill, a New Mexico horse breeder who had arrived at the ranch that morning to buy a colt looked across at Leigh. His pale blue eyes in the beefy face were frankly admiring beneath the bushy, sand-colored brows. Hemphill, although he had an air of boyish tomfoolery about him, was probably in his early fifties; metallic glints of silver in the sandy-brown hair were emphasized by the light from the dining-room chandelier. He had a rough, unpolished manner that was not softened by the expensive western suit and handmade boots he wore, as if his money—which, from the offhand way he'd chosen one of Shane's most expensive colts, he seemed to have in plenitude—was of recent acquisition.

"I don't see many good-looking gals out in the desert where my spread is," Hemphill continued jovially.

"You're very kind," Leigh said, aware of the amused glances from Shane and Rod. "I take it there is no Mrs. Hemphill?"

"Oh, no, ma'am. Not for over six years now. That's when my ex-wife and me decided to split the sheet, you might say."

"I see." Leigh toyed with a silver fork and sent a furtive glance in Rod's direction to her left, across the width of the dining table, which was attractively set with linen and silver and soft-beige ironstone.

She had a sense of having been railroaded into joining the three men for dinner. Shane had invited her in the presence of the other two—had grinned at Hemphill's obvious enthusiasm for the idea—and had sent her a look of

85

challenge over the New Mexico rancher's head. It had seemed, at the time, that she had little choice but to accept, and now she must make the best of it until politeness would allow her to excuse herself.

At the head of the table sat Shane in a cream-colored silk shirt that molded to the solid lines of his body like a second skin, and at his right was Rod in a pale blue shirt, also of silk. Across from Rod, Hemphill seemed overdressed in his brown western-style suit and loud brown-and-orange-striped necktie.

Maggie, assisted by María and the young Mexican girl Carmaleta, began to serve the salads—crisp fresh vegetables with Maggie's special Roquefort dressing. Leigh picked up her fork and tried to ignore the gray eyes that were resting on her from the other end of the table. She had been occupied with paperwork in the barn office the past few days and had, until now, managed to avoid much direct contact with her employer since that unnerving confrontation Monday afternoon.

"You don't seem to be very happy," Rod murmured, watching Leigh toy with the crisp lettuce in her salad bowl. "Wait till you see the main course. Rib-eye steaks marinated in wine and grilled with mushrooms over charcoal. It's another specialty of Maggie's."

"I—I think I'm just overtired." With a determined smile Leigh speared a chunk of tomato and popped it into her mouth.

Rod chuckled, leaning closer to say in a low voice, "You look as if you're forcing yourself to eat smelly raw fish instead of our home-grown tomatoes." He pushed the salad-dressing boat toward her. "Try a little more of this. No one can resist Maggie's dressing." He grinned conspiratorially. "Don't worry. Nobody would guess, by looking at you, that you'd rather not be here. You look cool and calm—and beautiful. That lavender dress does something for your eyes."

"You're a flatterer, Rod." Leigh took a little of the salad dressing for Maggie's sake.

Rod glanced toward the other two men, who were discussing the colt Hemphill had decided to buy. "You're only here to provide a little feminine diversion in this otherwise boring male company," he whispered. "Nobody expects you to entertain Hemphill. Besides, he's leaving in the morning, so don't let his rustic manners get on your nerves."

She gave him a slightly puzzled look, for she had actually forgotten Hemphill's presence for the moment. It was from Shane's nearness that she felt a longing to escape.

"Don't look so surprised." Rod chuckled softly. "Surely you've noticed our heavyset friend likes you. Not that I can blame him. Did I ever tell you your hair's the color of that pretty Texas wildflower that blooms in the spring?"

"Three or four times, at least. You shouldn't be so lavish with your compliments, Rod. No girl can take you seriously."

His look was suddenly grave. "In your case, I regret that."

Leigh gazed at him with uncertainty, unsure as to whether he was teasing or not. With Rod it was difficult to tell. Part of the time he was so absorbed in some obviously somber line of thought that he took little notice of other people. Then he would disappear from the house for several hours, or even overnight. At other times he was overly accommodating to her. She might have been able to believe his interest a serious one if he didn't usually manage at such times to mention Shane's refusal to allow him to sell his land. Obviously he hoped she would speak to Shane in his behalf. How very wrong he was if he imagined she could change his brother's mind on even the most inconsequential matter! And the selling of a single acre of Casey land was certainly not inconsequential, as far as Shane was concerned.

"If I could sell my land," Rod said now, almost as if he had been reading her thoughts, "I'd have a good amount of capital to invest in something more to my liking. I'd have something to recommend me to a woman then. It's not easy to live in Shane's shadow."

How very true that must be! Leigh's hand went to her throat to pull nervously at the small diamond teardrop that dangled from her gold necklace, a gift from her guardian, Jess Harlan.

She wondered now if Rod was hinting that it was she

87

for whom he felt the need of a recommendation? Oh, she was probably being too sensitive tonight. Still, she didn't want Rod to ask anything from her except friendship. She was sure it was all she could ever feel for him, no matter how charming or accommodating he might be. He just didn't appeal to her in an intimate way. He aroused no thrilling anticipation or bone-melting desire, things a woman ought to feel toward a man with whom she was considering forming a serious relationship.

"I swear, Shane, I don't know how you ever found a veterinarian who looks like this." Rex Hemphill's booming voice cut into Leigh's musing.

She could feel her nerves becoming taut as she became the focus of attention. "Leigh happens to be extremely conscientious," drawled Shane, giving her a lazy look. "In fact, Maggie chides me for overworking her."

"Maggie's right too," Rod put in. "Smith never worked half as hard as Leigh does."

Shane's attention was not diverted. "I saw Manuel leavin your apartment last night, Leigh. María tells me you were tutoring him in reading."

"Do you really think you can help him," Rod inquired.

"I can only try," she said.

Rod lifted his shoulders. "No wonder you're tired."

Shane spoke. "I haven't forgotten my promise about the books." He seemed to ponder for a moment before continuing. "You do look pale, Leigh. Carmaleta, pour Doctor Alexander a little more wine. Maybe that will put some color in her cheeks."

The Mexican girl obeyed, then followed Maggie from the dining room.

"It's probably due to the long hours I've been putting in on the horse records," Leigh remarked. "But I'm almost finished with them now. I plan to catch up on my rest this weekend."

"No trip planned?" Shane inquired unexpectedly. "Not even to San Antonio?"

"No."

"I'm relieved to hear it," Shane said. "You must sleep late Saturday, for a change."

Leigh longed to inform Shane that she could live without his feigned solicitousness; she hoped the swift look she gave him got the message across. When she saw his slight, sardonic smile, she knew he'd read her reaction perfectly. "Then you should be refreshed for our party Saturday evening." Shane's eyes rested on Leigh's tense face.

She felt resentment burning in her. What a clever devil he was! He'd tricked her into admitting, in front of witnesses, that she intended going nowhere Saturday. Now it seemed she had trapped herself. She could hardly refuse to attend the party after admitting she had nothing planned for the entire weekend.

"It's about time we had some people in," Rod was saying, his spirits clearly lightened by the prospect. "It's nearly the end of June and we haven't thrown a bash since the beginning of summer."

Shane's gaze continued to rest on Leigh for what seemed an endless moment. Then he swung around to Rod. "We've been somewhat remiss in our obligations, I'm afraid. I've a long list of friends whose hospitality needs repaying. Some of them will be coming for swimming early—about three—and then Maggie is planning one of her incomparable barbecues for eighty on the patio."

"Shucks, it sounds like a rip-roaring good time," boomed Hemphill. "A crying shame I have to get back to New Mexico tomorrow."

Maggie and María brought in the steaks and baked potatoes at that moment. When the serving was finished, Shane said smoothly, "We regret that you won't be able to join us Saturday, Rex."

Leigh knew this to be an untruth since Shane's impatience with the robust rancher had been apparent to her several times. Oh, how easily he lied!

"You've never been to a barbecue, Leigh," Rod said with a twinkle in his eye, "until you've been to a Texas barbecue."

"If I'm feeling rested enough to attend," Leigh said. "If not, I'm certain I won't be missed."

"On the contrary." Shane's eyes narrowed as they dwelt on her face. "You will be the feature attraction. Our friends are looking forward to meeting you."

"I can't imagine why," she protested, glancing away from him.

"Our lives are rather routine," he said, but the gleam in his eyes denied that *his* life fit into that category. "You are something of a novelty, Leigh."

"If you mean because of my profession," she said, bridling, "that's nonsense."

"I wasn't referring merely to your profession," Shane remarked enigmatically as he cut into his steak.

"Don't be nervous about meeting so many strangers all at once," Rod said. "I'll keep an eye on you. Besides, we're a friendly lot around here. You'll feel among friends in no time."

Leigh doubted that. After all, Shane would be there—and Phyllis Calhoun. She turned her attention to her steak, which was everything Rod had led her to expect. It was her appetite that was not up to par. She felt as if she had to force down every mouthful of the succulent beef and sour-cream-drenched baked potato.

After the main course, a frothy peaches-and-whipped-cream dessert was served with coffee. Normally, Leigh found sweet foods to her liking, but at the moment the sight of the gleaming peach slices and rich white cream made her feel slightly ill.

She was suddenly aware of Maggie hovering at her elbow. "Is there anything wrong with your dessert, Leigh?"

Leigh looked up at her apologetically. "No, it's delicious, but I'm too full to eat another bite. Could you save it for me until tomorrow?"

Maggie nodded and removed the dessert, carrying it from the dining room. Leigh folded her napkin beside her plate. "If you gentlemen will excuse me—"

The three men got to their feet as she rose. "Sure you wouldn't like to go for a little stroll after dinner?" Hemphill asked hopefully. "Or maybe the four of us could have a nice friendly game of cards."

"Thank you, but not tonight," Leigh said.

"I'll accommodate you with a card game," Rod offered.

"Shane," she heard Hemphill saying, as she left the room, "I reckon you'll be coming out to New Mexico in the fall for the Futurity."

90

"Naturally." Shane's voice drifted after Leigh down the hall. "I hope to have a horse in the race."

Hemphill's response to this was lost on Leigh as she entered her apartment. She was grateful that Manuel wasn't coming for a reading session tonight. After trying to help him the previous evening with the aid of a children's magazine she'd picked up off the rack at a store in San Lorenzo, she had decided to wait for the grade-level books Shane had promised her. She took a shower and got into a thin summer nightgown before propping herself up in bed to read a novel.

It must have been about an hour later when there was a knock at her door. "Just a minute," she called as she reached for her white nylon robe and, tying it around her, went into the living room to open the door.

It was Shane. "I brought the books for Manuel." He carried a stack in the crook of one elbow. "May I come in?"

Reluctantly she stepped back. He put the books on a lamp table and turned back to her. "I really think you may be taking on too much with these reading lessons, Leigh."

"Someone has to help Manuel," she replied stubbornly.

"Phyllis seems to think you may make matters worse."

"Well, that's about what I expected from her," she retorted.

He took a few steps toward her. He looked so tall in his dark trousers and cream-colored shirt. An extremely attractive man, she had to admit; but now she imagined there was something threatening in the set of his shoulders and in the darkening of his eyes. He moved almost stealthily, like some predatory animal.

"You're being unfair, Leigh." He loomed above her and there was no mistaking the impatience in the hard lines of his face. "Why don't you admit that you want to prove Phyllis wrong—just because it's Phyllis."

If Leigh were to be perfectly honest, she could not deny that his accusation might contain a grain of truth. But beyond that she really did believe that Phyllis was wrong about Manuel. "I want to prove Phyllis wrong for Manuel's sake," she said firmly.

"That's what I told her," he remarked, "but I don't think she believed me."

"I'm sure you made her think I have some personal grudge against her!" She glared up into his tanned face. "Do you enjoy taunting women when you know they care for you as Phyllis does?"

"Don't tell me about Phyllis Calhoun!" His jaw tightened. "She has no ties on me. I've made that very clear."

Leigh fought down the slight flutter in the pit of her stomach that felt like relief—but could not be. "Why does she dislike Manuel?"

He scowled darkly and looked beyond her shoulder for a moment. "I don't know. She's not an easy woman to understand. But there are the tests." He looked back to Leigh's face. "They have repeatedly shown the boy to be far below average in intelligence."

The tests! It always came back to the tests. If she were to convince the school board, she would have to produce other test results to back up her position. She moved to the couch and sat down suddenly, raking slender fingers through the waves of her hair. "The tests are wrong, Shane. I know they are."

He sat down beside her and when she looked up, she saw that he was smiling. "A typical female reaction, based entirely on emotion. You've taken a liking to Manuel, so he has to be perfect."

Wordlessly she shook her head, her hair falling down in careless disarray. "I'm going to fight Phyllis if I have to."

He looked down at her, at her hair tumbling half across her face, at the soft creamy skin of her neck and the portion of her shoulders that was exposed in the gaping neck of her robe and the plunging gown beneath. His face was lean, the cheeks seemingly chiseled from stone, and she felt a pulse beating furiously at her temple during the silence that hung between them.

When his hand reached out to push at her falling hair and cup her face, she could not seem to gather enough strength to move away. "You don't have to fight me to fight Phyllis," he said softly. His mouth came down on hers searchingly, parting her lips. An ache had invaded her body, starting deep inside her and spreading to every cell, a tormenting sort of yearning against which she had no defense. She could not deny that she wanted him to go on kissing her, drawing out that sweet torture, sending fire along the skin of her neck in the wake of his wandering lips. What he had said that day in the barn was true. *You won't always fight me, Leigh . . . you don't want to.* She longed to ignore Phyllis Calhoun and whatever she was to Shane and, throwing caution to the wind, obey her own treacherous emotions.

"Leigh . . . oh, Leigh. . . ." His voice vibrated softly against the curve of her shoulder where he had pushed the robe aside. The words brushed deep and sure across her most sensitive nerves. She felt a languid warmth creeping over her. She could not stop his searching lips, the sensual movement of his fingers as they explored the curves of her body. She couldn't want to.

A sharp rap at the door brought her back to reality. "Leigh, is Shane in there?" It was Rod's voice. "He's wanted on the phone. Phyllis Calhoun."

"Tell her I'll call her back later," Shane growled, his eyes devouring Leigh's face.

Now that his lips were not in contact with her skin, she summoned enough strength to move away from him, to stand. "You'd better go take your call," she said bitterly.

"Leigh, it's not important."

Suddenly she was furious, remembering the night he had taken Phyllis home after the day in San Antonio, the night when he had not returned until after she was sound asleep. She heard again Phyllis's taunting words implying that Shane was a demanding lover. "Will you deny that she's your mistress?" she said in a breaking voice.

He got to his feet, the gray eyes, which had only seconds before softened as he looked into her face, were now hard and angry. "I will neither confirm nor deny that, Leigh, because it has nothing to do with you." With that, he walked away from her, jerked open the door, and shut it loudly behind him.

The sun was still brilliant in the western sky and awesome in its power and majesty. Sounds mingled in the

93

courtyard—laughter and idle chatter, ice tinkling in glasses, water splashing from the pool. Leigh paused at the edge of the patio and watched the Caseys' guests lounging on the turf at the edge or playing in the clear blue-green water. She had been introduced to all of them during the afternoon, but there were too many names to remember all at once. Rod had led her from one clump of guests to the next, and then, without explanation, he had disappeared. She hadn't seen him for half an hour and had decided to go change to her swimsuit. Not the bikini this time. This was a brown one-piece suit cut low in back but high enough in front for modesty.

Most of the women were far more tanned than she, although her fair skin had taken on a golden glow since her arrival at the ranch. These were the pool-loungers Shane had told her about, the wives of his friends, who spent their days in idleness. She walked toward the pool.

"Hi, honey." The greeting came from a chunky blonde with friendly green eyes. She was sitting at the shallow end of the pool in a white bikini, her feet dangling in the water, a can of beer in one hand. Rod had introduced Leigh to her and her husband earlier. Mary something. . . .

"Sit down here and visit with me." Mary patted the turf beside her. "My husband's gone somewhere with Rod."

Leigh sat down and was immediately approached by one of the Mexican ranch hands who had been pressed into service for the day as a waiter. Several of them were circulating among the guests with trays of drinks.

"Would you like a drink, Doctor Alexander?"

Leigh looked over the contents of his tray. "A ginger ale, please." He opened the frosty can, handed it to her, and moved away.

"I can't imagine where Rod has gone," Leigh said.

Mary's green eyes regarded her curiously for a moment before she laughed. "Law, honey, I can. He and my husband and a few of the other men have got a card game going somewhere. I told Larry I'd leave if he got into a game today." She shrugged good-naturedly. "But he never listens to me. I decided to stay, though, and enjoy myself." She grinned mischievously and gestured for one of the waiters to bring her another beer. "Larry has his little pleasures, and I have mine."

Leigh looked out over the pool, which teemed with tanned bodies in all shapes and sizes. At the deep end she saw Shane dunking a squealing Phyllis and quickly glanced away. "I can't believe they'd leave a party like this just to play cards."

Mary shook her head and peered toward the ranch house. Its dark red roof tiles glowed like copper, its white walls gleamed in the sunlight. Her eyes narrowed. "Wait'll you get married, honey. Men will leave anything to play cards. *Some* men, anyway." She was gazing toward the deep end of the pool now where Shane and Phyllis were cavorting. "Why couldn't I have married somebody like Shane Casey? Now *he'd* never leave his guests for a card game. He's too well-mannered."

Leigh had to admit that Shane had played the gracious host to perfection ever since the first guest had arrived almost two hours earlier. Only a short while ago, at Phyllis's repeated urgings, had he agreed to leave his duties temporarily to go into the pool. It had taken Phyllis almost two hours to get Shane's full attention, but she had finally managed it. As Leigh had noticed on previous occasions Phyllis Calhoun was a relentless woman. She had hardly left Shane's side since the party began.

"Now that," continued Mary, a devilish twinkle in her eye, "is a sexy man." She glanced at Leigh and giggled. "Honey, did you know you're blushing? I guess you've noticed too, huh?"

Leigh took a long swallow of ginger ale to cover her confusion. "My job keeps me too busy to speculate about things like that."

Mary whooped. "*Sure* it does! But listen to an older and wiser head, honey. Don't get any bright ideas. I'd hate to see you tangle with Phyllis Calhoun. She fights dirty."

"I've no intention of tangling with Phyllis," Leigh said primly. "Not over Shane Casey, at any rate." She would, however, she thought with an inward shrinking, likely have to do battle with the woman over Manuel. She had made up her mind to take the boy somewhere for a series of aptitude and intelligence tests. She had worked with Manuel

95

several evenings during the past week, and already she thought she could detect a slight improvement in his reading. But it would take more than that to convince the school board that he shouldn't be removed from the regular class. She would have to have the parents' permission for new tests, of course, but the right moment to broach the subject hadn't presented itself. And time was running out. The school board meeting was little more than two weeks away now.

"Oh, look, there are a couple of empty lounges." Mary's words interrupted Leigh's thoughts. "Let's grab them before somebody else does."

Leigh followed the short, chunky woman willingly away from the pool. She lay beside Mary on one of the redwood lounges. Mary had had her third beer since Leigh joined her, and Leigh wondered how many she had had before that, for her words were beginning to slur.

Shortly Mary got to her feet, swaying slightly. "I've got to go to the little girl's room, honey. See you later."

Leigh shaded her eyes with one hand and peered up at the woman. "Need any help?"

Mary giggled. "You think I'm drunk, don't you? Well, don't you worry about little ol' me." She started slowly toward the house.

"She's had too much to drink, as usual." The scornful voice belonged to Phyllis Calhoun. Leigh turned to see the redhead, wearing a sky-blue bikini that displayed her voluptuous curves to excellent advantage, looking after the swaying Mary. Shane stood beside her, rubbing his arms with a towel.

He turned away, for a moment, to bring a third lounge over and then he took the one next to Leigh, leaving a lounge for Phyllis on his other side.

Phyllis was lathering herself with suntan lotion. She had the sort of skin that did not take the sun well. "You better put some of this on too, Leigh," Phyllis said as she finished with her legs. "You're going to burn." She recapped the plastic bottle and tossed it onto the turf near Leigh's lounge.

Leigh retrieved it and began spreading the lotion on her arms. "Thanks. I forgot to bring mine out with me."

Phyllis sat on the edge of her lounge and watched Leigh. Between them, Shane reclined, his thick, dark lashes lowered.

"I'm surprised you're not further along on a tan," Phyllis remarked, and Leigh noticed, for, the first time, the brittle edge of her tone. "Since you have the convenience of a pool."

"My work doesn't leave a lot of time for enjoying the pool."

"Oh, I keep forgetting. You *do* work here, don't you?" There was definitely antagonism in Phyllis's manner. Why? Leigh wondered. Was it merely the fact that she, Leigh, lived at the ranch and saw Shane every day? Or was Phyllis angry with Shane about something and taking it out on the nearest scapegoat?

"I'm not as fortunate as you are," Leigh said, pretending not to notice the fire smoldering in the tawny eyes. "I don't have the summers off."

"And I don't have a pool," Phyllis retorted peevishly. "I have to wait until I'm invited to use this one. I've been informed I mustn't drop in unexpectedly any more." She glanced quickly at Shane's long, tan body sprawled on the lounge beside her. Suddenly he opened his eyes and caught her look. In the silence that followed, something passed between the dark man and the red-haired woman that caused Leigh to shiver.

Phyllis flounced full-length on the lounge. "You're not being a very good host, darling. I'd like to have a drink."

Leigh concentrated on applying lotion to her legs.

"José or one of the other men at the bar will be glad to get you whatever you want, Phyllis." Shane's voice was low, but there was no mistaking the steel underlying the measured words.

Phyllis sat upright again. "In the way of a drink, you mean! Oh, all right." She tried to laugh, but it didn't come off convincingly. "After all, I'm really not a guest, am I? Would you like something, darling?"

"Not now, thank you," Shane said curtly.

Phyllis moved away jerkily, fury stiffening her spine.

Shane watched her retreating back for a moment, then turned to Leigh. "Lie down," he directed. "I'll get your back." Momentarily she considered refusing, but that would make it appear as if she considered his offer something more than a friendly gesture. Besides, she couldn't reach her back and, even though the sun was low, if her skin wasn't protected, it would burn quickly.

She handed him the bottle and lay down on her stomach, resting her cheek on her arms, and closed her eyes. His hand touched her shoulder and a permeating warmth radiated from the contact. Leigh tried to force her mind to think of something else, anything to keep her mind off the slow, intimate movement of Shane's hand as it traced the contours of her back caressingly.

"Your skin is like silk, Leigh." The words were spoken softly near her ear.

Her eyes flew open and she saw him bent over her, the dark lashes swept low over the gray eyes, the late-afternoon sun touching the planes of his face in a way that created stark shadows along the hard cheekbones. The strong fingers massaged along her backbone, lingering for a long, heart-stopping moment on the small of her back where her swimsuit began, and then they traveled to one side, working their way sensuously up to her shoulder blade.

"You feel as a beautiful woman should feel," the husky voice continued, "soft and yielding to a man's touch."

"You—you can stop now," she said breathlessly. "I think you've taken care of my back adequately. I'm protected now."

There was a soft laugh and his hand slipped down, resting against the curve of her breast. Even through the fabric of her swimsuit it burned like a hot branding iron. "From the sun, yes. Ah, but I find I have an almost uncontrollable desire to touch more than your back, Leigh. Unfortunately we'd have an audience. I don't think you are the sort of woman who makes love in public."

She turned over and sat up abruptly. "Nor anywhere else—with you!"

"Why do you fight your feelings?" he inquired softly, with maddening calm. "I am no teen-ager, Leigh. I know when a woman wants me to make love to her."

"Oh, you're very experienced!" Something in her had to

lash out at him in anger, to protect her heart. She was a challenge to Shane, nothing more. He saw her as a game to be won, a horse to be broken, a woman to be subdued. Her stomach twisted as the hard look came back into his eyes. For a moment she had an insane desire to touch him, to invite his caresses once more, to plead with him to take her to some secret place and make her feel that bittersweet torture again. If they had been alone, she knew with swift certainty, nothing could have stopped the explosion that was igniting between them.

The clenched jaw relaxed slowly. "Don't look so frightened. I'll not ravish you in front of fifty guests." He glanced away from her, letting his gaze travel over the pool. "Not that this wouldn't be a setting conducive to romance, especially by moonlight." His gaze rested once more on her face. "I can imagine the scene quite clearly, can't you, Leigh?"

Seemingly of its own volition, Leigh's hand went to her throat, pressing itself against the heat of her skin. The naive little girl from the sheltered college campus, she thought, who wouldn't be able to resist the mysterious fascination of this giant of a Texan in whom were mingled the toughness of the western frontier and the passions of the wild Irish moors. Was any woman safe from him?

Her eyes fled away from his intense scrutiny. "They're setting up the tables on the patio," she said, grasping at the diversion as a drowning man lunges for a life preserver. She ran the tip of her tongue over dry lips. "I—I think I'll go in and change before dinner." Without looking at him again, she walked hurriedly across the warm pavement and entered the coolness of the house. Once inside her apartment she stood with her back against the closed door, breathing deeply to calm her pounding heart. Now calm reason could surface again. He had no right to talk to her as he had done! He was a practiced wooer of women, she told herself angrily, whose lying words flowed easily from that shallow region where desire had no contact with the heart.

She moved slowly across the living room and entered her bedroom which was shady and cool because of the drawn draperies. She switched on the light and stood in front of the mirror . . . staring at herself, at the heightened color—which was not from the sun—that still lingered in her cheeks, at the longing gleam in her blue-violet eyes beneath the tumbled, sun-bleached hair. She could still feel his hand against her skin, the power that emanated from his strong fingers—fingers that could hurt tender skin or coax resistant emotions to passionate heights.

It was physical attraction, desire to experience the pleasures of the flesh, and had absolutely nothing to do with love or trust or any other abiding emotion. As she lifted the heavy weight of her hair off her neck, she remembered again the night he had come to her apartment to bring Manuel's books, and the deep vibration of his voice against her bare shoulder, repeating her name. Gazing at her reflection in the mirror, she could not deny the desire in her eyes to have the experience repeated. Why must she remember those times whenever their eyes met? Why not remember, instead, the stubborn strength of his will, his pride and arrogance? Let other women pursue him. She would not lower herself to their level. And then she would not be left, as they, with nothing but a broken heart and shattered dreams.

With resolution she turned away from her reflection and went into the bathroom to shower. Afterward she dressed in a pale lilac-colored halter-top sundress and high-heeled sandals with narorw white straps. She pulled her hair back and wound it in an intricate roll at the back of her head, securing it with combs embedded with pale lavender amethysts.

She left the apartment and went along the darkened hall in the direction of the kitchen, thinking that perhaps she could be of help to Maggie. But before she reached the kitchen, she came upon María standing alone in the hall, her head bowed.

"María?" she questioned softly. "Is anything wrong?"

When the Mexican woman raised her head, Leigh saw that tears shimmered in her dark brown eyes. "What is it, María? Can I help?"

María shook her head, wiping her eyes with the tail of her white apron. "No, Doctor Leigh. Nobody can help. I'll get used to the idea. Only, does she have to remind me of it every time she comes here?"

"Who? Remind you of what?"

"That woman!" María's shimmering eyes glinted angrily. "Miss Calhoun. Every time she comes here, she finds a way to get me alone and tell me Manuel is—retarded. The school board is going to put my boy in that special class. Miss Calhoun said they would say so at the next meeting. And then José and I will get a letter."

"María, listen to me." Urgency hardened Leigh's tone, strengthened her resolve. "You cannot accept this. You have to fight her."

María's large brown eyes widened. "Fight her? Fight a teacher? Oh, no, Doctor Leigh. She is educated. She has many tests to show to the school board. She must know what she is talking about."

Leigh saw in María the same awe for the teaching profession that she had seen in José. In their scheme of values teachers were evidently held in high regard, not to be questioned or doubted. "But you know your son, María," Leigh persisted. "You know in your heart that Manuel is a normal little boy."

María shook her head helplessly. "I don't know what to think—" Her voice broke.

"I've been with him a lot the last week or so," Leigh went on. "It's true he doesn't read as well as he should, but that is far from being retarded. I want to take him to San Antonio, María. Have him tested there by experts. I will help you fight this thing."

María only stared at her, speechless with fright and uncertainty.

"There has to be something behind this," Leigh said thoughtfully. "Does Phyllis Calhoun have any reason to dislike you or José? Perhaps she is taking out an old grudge against you by persecuting your son."

María's head went back and forth slowly. "I can think of no reason. I know that she hates me, though. I see it in her eyes when she looks at me. But I do not know why. I have sometimes thought it is because I am Mexican. Maybe she is prejudiced against my race."

It was Leigh's turn to shake her head. "Even if that were true, it doesn't seem enough to explain her determination to get Manuel out of her classroom. Surely he isn't the only Mexican child in the third grade."

"No," María agreed. "There are others. At least twelve or thirteen, I think."

"Are any of them scheduled to go into the special class?"

"No. Only Manuel."

Leigh looked into María's sad eyes. "Let me take Manuel for the tests next Saturday."

The sadness was joined now with fear. "I don't know, Doctor Leigh. I will have to talk to José about it."

"All right. But, María, try to make him see that Manuel's future may depend on it."

María nodded silently, and the two walked back to the kitchen together. Leigh left her there pondering the revolutionary suggestion that she defy her son's teacher.

SEVEN

Leigh's first look at the lavishly spread buffet table confirmed Rod's promise that a Texas barbecue was like no other. There were huge trays loaded with melon balls, grapes, plums, and sliced fresh peaches, pineapple, and bananas. More trays held homemade Mexican cornbread, white bread, and fluffy rolls. Banquet-sized bowls contained *tabouleh*, cole slaw, and at least a dozen different kinds of salads. Deep stainless-steel tubs held barbecued beef, chicken, and ham—all laced with a delicious spicy sauce made from a secret recipe that Maggie steadfastly refused to reveal to the many female guests who asked.

Japanese lanterns were strung across the patio, and redwood tables and folding chairs were scattered about. When the serving had started, Rod had reappeared at Leigh's elbow and they stood together in the buffet line.

"Is your card game over?" she inquired.

The question seemed to take Rod by surprise. "Yes—but how did you know that's what I was doing?"

"One of the women—Mary something—told me. Actually she wasn't very happy about your appropriating her husband."

Rod's face darkened as he looked across the patio where Mary and her balding husband stood in another line. "She's probably happy now. Larry cleaned the rest of us out."

So the card game had been serious gambling. Leigh had wondered before if money was involved in the game. From Rod's cloudy look, quite a bit had been at stake.

When they'd filled their plates, they found a table and were soon joined by the blonde Mary, who seemed sober

103

now, and her husband. A few minutes later Shane and Phyllis sat down at their table too.

Shane wore tan trousers and a pale green knit shirt. Phyllis hadn't bothered to change from her bikini, but had simply donned a floor-length wraparound skirt in the same shade of blue and added a blue flower to her shining copper-colored hair. She looked ravishing, Leigh admitted to herself.

Larry was in good spirits as he attacked his overflowing plate. "Shane, I couldn't draw anything but winning hands tonight."

Rod squirmed uncomfortably at the man's words and looked down at his plate. Leigh's brief glance at Shane told her he was angry about something.

"How come you never will play with us?" Larry continued, looking at Shane, seemingly unaware of the undercurrents at the table.

"I'm not a gambling man, Larry," Shane retorted tersely.

"Now that's hard to believe," Larry exclaimed. "You raise racing quarter horses, don't you?"

"I raise them and race them, Larry," Shane said, "but I don't bet on them. I leave that to more reckless heads."

Larry looked nonplussed. "You mean you don't bet on your own horses?"

Shane returned shortly. "The quarter-horse business has enough uncertainties without adding gambling to the list."

"Golly," Mary squealed, "how can you resist when you get to the track, with all that excitement and everything? Come on, Shane, fess up. Don't you place a little impulsive bet once in a while?"

"Mary, you ought to know by now," Rod put in tonelessly, "that Shane does nothing on impulse. All of his actions are carefully calculated. Everything based on estimated profit and loss."

"And there is even less possibility of predicting the outcome of a card game than of a horse race," Shane cut in. "A fact that on occasion might be profitably recalled by others."

Leigh sensed the tensing muscles of the man who sat

beside her. *"Profitably!"* Rod's voice was openly scornful now. "Precisely my point, Shane."

Others at the table were becoming uncomfortable in the face of the obvious antagonism between the brothers. "Come now, kiddies," Phyllis said into the thick silence that had descended. "Mother will send you to your rooms if you don't behave."

Mary giggled, and the tension lessened noticeably. "Hurry and eat, Larry, honey. They're starting to dance."

Leigh glanced toward the far end of the courtyard, where several couples were drifting onto the tiled floor. Stereo equipment had been moved onto the patio and the mellow quadrophonic sounds of "You Light Up My Life" drifted on the balmy summer evening air.

Rod pushed his half-eaten food aside. "Dance with me, Leigh?"

She nodded, glad for any excuse to leave the table, where Mary and Larry were casting romantic glances at each other, Phyllis sat with half-exposed breasts, smiling an enigmatic smile, and Shane still scowled darkly.

When they reached the section of the courtyard set aside for dancing, Rod took Leigh into his arms and led her easily into a slow fox-trot. He seemed to be making an effort to throw off his earlier dour mood. "When they put on the disco tunes," he said apologetically, "I'm afraid I'll have to retire to the spectators' section."

"That's fine," Leigh assured him. "I prefer the slower dances myself."

He looked down at her as he swung her about smoothly. "I'll bet you can disco, though. Isn't that what they do at college these days?"

"Mostly. And I've done it a few times, but I certainly couldn't win any contests."

He held her comfortably, not too close, and she found that, in spite of his deprecating words, he was a good dancer.

After a bit Rod said, "I'm sorry for leaving you in the lurch earlier. Were you able to entertain yourself?"

"Quite well. I talked with Mary for a while and a few other guests too. Then I had to change, of course. And I had a talk with María."

Rod pulled his head back to look down at her. "María Gomez?"

"Yes. I ran into her in the hall as I was coming out to eat. She was crying, Rod."

Rod's expression told her nothing. "Not from peeling onions, I take it."

"No. As I said, she was standing in the hall, trying to stop crying, I suppose, before she returned to the kitchen. When I asked what was wrong, I learned that Phyllis had been talking to her about Manuel."

Rod let out a long breath. "I see."

"Honestly I don't understand that woman. She seems to *enjoy* telling the Gomezes that their son isn't doing well in school. At least that's what María believes. Phyllis has it in for that boy and his family, I think." She was silent for a moment, remembering María's helpless tears earlier. "Where did they live before they came to the ranch?"

"The Gomezes? José came out from San Antonio as a young man to work on a neighboring ranch. María was raised here. Her parents worked for my father."

"Phyllis has known María for some time then."

"In a manner of speaking." Rod laughed shortly. "Phyllis usually doesn't deign to notice the existence of servants."

"Yes, I would have guessed that. Which makes it doubly strange that she seems to have developed a grudge against the Gomezes. What did they ever do to her?"

Rod was smiling quizzically. "Didn't María tell you?"

Leigh looked up at him intently. "She doesn't know why Phyllis dislikes Manuel."

"Is that what she told you?"

"Yes, and it was obviously the truth." When Rod did not respond, she went on. "What was María like, growing up?"

His shoulders lifted slightly. "I know it's hard to believe it now, but she was a beauty as a young girl. All the young Mexican men in the neighborhood were after her. Even a few of the Anglos. You should have seen her at seventeen. I must confess I had a few daydreams about her myself." He laughed again. "Of course, I wouldn't have done anything about it." When Leigh smiled doubtfully, he said, "Oh, you can believe it. Her father was fiercely protective. That old man scared the pants off me. I was never as bold as Shane. But María married José when she was eighteen and, as far as I know, she's been a dutiful wife ever since." Was there an undertone of mockery in the last comment? Was he implying that after her marriage María had undergone a change of character? That before the wedding she had been less circumspect?

"She still has beautiful eyes. I can believe that she must have been lovely as a young girl."

He shook his head, smiling as if she'd said something funny. "Obviously you've heard some of the local gossip."

The music had stopped momentarily and he followed her to the edge of the dance floor, where she turned to face him. "I don't know what you mean by 'local gossip.' Has it something to do with María? Something that would explain Phyllis's dislike of her and her son?"

It was shadowy where they stood, and she could not see his face clearly. "Ranches are like small towns, Leigh. People know each other well—maybe too well—and life can get boring. So they carry tales. It adds a little spice to the monotony. But it doesn't really matter whether something that was whispered about eight or nine years ago was real or only imagined, does it? It's ancient history now."

She had no idea what he was talking about. "That depends. Some things affect people and those close to them for years, even for generations."

The stereo was blasting out a fast, snappy disco tune now. Rod stared off into the darkness beyond the courtyard, his hands in his pockets. "If you have enough money, almost anything can be forgotten."

"What?"

"Hey, Leigh, come on and let's show 'em a thing or two." Larry, Rod's card-playing partner, was standing in front of her, grinning devilishly. There was a strong smell of whiskey on his breath. "Mary won't try the fast ones."

She looked at Rod, who shrugged. Having no other choice, she followed the overweight Larry to the dance floor, where he grabbed her and surprised her by being a more than passable disco dancer. She was soon gasping for breath, but Larry was enjoying their dance so much, she had to laugh. "You've been practicing," she said above the noise of the stereo.

He winked broadly as he swayed away from her for a moment before catching her about the waist and swinging her under his arm. "Don't tell Mary," he panted, as he set her on her feet again. "She thinks I have a natural talent. She doesn't know I go discoing whenever I take a load of cattle to the sale in Fort Worth."

When the music stopped, Leigh started for the sidelines, grateful for the respite. But before she'd gone three steps, the strains of another slow tune poured forth and Larry grabbed her again. "Just one more dance, Leigh, before Mary gets back from wherever she went." When she held back, he coaxed, "Aw, come on."

She gave in and they'd danced only a few seconds before Shane cut in. When they had moved away from Larry, he said, "I thought you might want rescuing."

She had been wondering how to extricate herself from Larry's overzealous embrace, but being in Shane's arms wasn't her idea of a rescue! "He's had a little too much to drink, I think."

"So's his wife," Shane said dryly. "Maggie put her to bed in one of the guest rooms. It seems she was sick all over the bathroom floor."

"I talked to her earlier. She's unhappy."

"Unhappily married, you mean? That seems to be the case with too many of my friends. I've often wondered what goes wrong."

When the tune came to an end, another slow melody started without pause. Her heart fluttering, she wondered if Shane had somehow managed that. His hand pressed firmly at her waist, holding her body tightly against his hard-muscled strength. She felt his warm breath mingling with her hair.

She attempted to keep the conversation going. "Too many people rush into marriage on the basis of . . . physical attraction alone."

She thought she heard a soft chuckle. When she tried to

pull back so that she could look up at him, he held her too tightly. "Oh, go ahead and make fun," she said through clenched teeth, her head pressed into the hollow of his neck, "but I think that husband and wife should be more than lovers. They should be friends too—have interests in common."

"I'm not making fun," he said calmly. "I happen to agree with you."

"Oh, really? I was under the impression you didn't think highly of marriage under any circumstances."

He chuckled again. "What I have seen hasn't given me much encouragement to do otherwise."

"What—where are you taking me?" She was suddenly aware that he had led her to the edge of the dance floor and beyond. They were now in a dark corner formed by the angle of the high courtyard wall, obscured from view by a large rubber plant. Leigh found herself with her back to the wall and Shane's arms imprisoning her on either side.

"You are quite right, little one." His voice was deep and soft, like satin drawn across tender nerves, and the pale light from a distant lantern caught in his dark lashes and shadowed his gray eyes so that they appeared like shining ebony. Though she felt trapped, Leigh wanted to reach out and trace the clean angles of his face.

"I—I don't know what you mean." She managed to keep her voice steady, but the strength of will required to keep her hand from rising to his face was such that it came as a shock to her.

"Physical attraction isn't everything between a man and a woman," he said huskily, "but on the other hand . . ."

"Yes?" Leigh bit her lip.

"Without it, everything else is ashes." He moved slowly, almost languidly, to take her face in his warm hands.

He forced her chin up so that she had to look into his eyes, and he was gazing back at her, his eyes dark and luminous in the shadow of his black brows. "Don't you agree?"

"Of course." She lowered her lashes, closing out the sight of his handsome face so close to her own. For the first time she wondered if she could be in love with him. Was love this mixture of nervous quaking and bittersweet longing? She had the unnerving feeling, as his eyes swept over her face in a look that was as intimate as a kiss, that she was at the same time in danger and protected by his strength.

With a soft growl he pulled her to him and she could feel the sensuous heat of his mouth against the skin of her forehead. She wanted to reach up and run her hands through his dark hair, to feel the hard muscles at the back of his neck and across his broad shoulders and back.

His lips moved against her skin, causing a flame of yearning to erupt inside her. "You are the most desirable—and the most maddening—woman I have ever known."

He moved his head back enough to look down into her face. Silently they regarded each other for a long moment.

"Shane, please—"

With a fierce movement he brought his mouth down against hers and kissed her until her will was no longer strong enough to keep her arms from clasping tightly around him. The world was lost to her; they might as well have been alone on an island. There was nothing but the feel of his lips, his arms. When his hand slid to the halter top of her dress and caressed the soft fullness of her breast, her heart leaped and a soft sigh of pleasure formed deep in her throat.

His fingers traced the outlines of her body as he buried his lips in the softness of her neck. "Why do you keep punishing us like this? Our bodies were made for each other, my beautiful Leigh."

She closed her eyes and felt a hot pricking of tears against her eyelids as his words washed over her, stabbing her heart. *Our bodies,* he had said. *But what of our souls,* she cried inside, *what of our hearts?* She drew a shuddering breath. "Because I know I would hate myself afterward—and you as well."

He lifted his head. "Those are the words of a very young girl," he said sadly. "You don't know what you're saying. You would not hate me afterward. I think I could make you feel something quite different from that."

"No, Shane." The tremor in the words revealed her inner wavering, however. Could he sense her weakness?

"I want to see you later, after everyone has gone. I will come to your apartment."

"No," she repeated.

For a brief moment, as his arms still held her, his eyes met hers, smoldering with desire. "I will come," he said, and then he let her go and moved away from her toward the dancing couples.

She stood with her back against the courtyard wall, her hands pressed against the rough stucco, the deep throbbing from the stereo keeping time with the throb of her heart. She wasn't certain if it was love she felt for Shane; she only knew that whenever they were alone, whenever they came close to each other, a magic kind of electricity was in the air and, no matter what resolutions she had made previously, nothing seemed important but the sight and feel of him.

Her fingers moved slowly over the roughness of the stucco wall, and she admitted that she wished they were still moving over Shane's back and through his hair. The aroma that was specially his still hung over her—a combination of warm, masculine skin, clean-smelling soap, the faint smell of the occasional cheroots he smoked, and a tinge of his musky after-shave. She had never met anyone like Shane Casey before and somehow she knew that she never would again.

A few minutes later, when she left her concealed corner, Shane was not in sight. She moved along the perimeter of the courtyard, keeping to the shadows. She reached the back door of the house and stepped inside.

"I've been looking for you." Phyllis Calhoun stood in the lighted hallway, and her slanting, tawny eyes took in Leigh's startled look with no attempt to conceal her contempt. Had Phyllis seen her and Shane together?

"What is it?"

"María tells me you think Manuel should be tested

111

again—by someone besides me." The full, sensuous lips curled around the words.

"I made that suggestion, yes."

Leigh noticed that Phyllis's hands were clasped tightly at her sides. "You are really full of bright ideas, aren't you? First you go after Shane, and now this."

"I have not 'gone after Shane,' as you put it."

Phyllis's laugh was mocking, mirthless. "Oh, I'm certain you're making him think he's the aggressor. I don't happen to be so easily fooled. You're nothing but a scheming little—"

Leigh felt her anger flaming in her face. "I do not intend to continue this conversation, Phyllis." She moved to pass the other woman.

"Oh, but you will!" Phyllis blocked her way. She could not pass without shoving the other woman aside, an act which would snatch away whatever shreds of dignity she was managing to hold on to in this encounter.

She faced Phyllis squarely. "Since you seem determined to talk, perhaps you will answer a question. Why are you trying to have Manuel removed from your class?"

"Not only trying, *Doctor* Alexander," she sneered. "It shall be accomplished. In fact, it has already been accomplished, except for the formality of the school board's approval."

"Are you sure you have tested him thoroughly?"

Phyllis's tawny eyes flashed indignant sparks. "How dare you question my professional judgment!" Her voice quivered with rage.

"My questions are legitimate, Phyllis. Isn't it true that the tests you've given Manuel are in English?"

"Of course they're in English! What did you think they'd be in? Bantu?"

Leigh made an effort to keep her tone calm and reasonable. "I thought they might be in Spanish."

"Spanish! All our classes are conducted in English. Why should the tests be in another language?"

"Because," said Leigh, straining for patience, "you are dealing with a child from a Spanish-speaking home. Surely you at least read the test questions aloud to him."

"The test is designed partly to determine how well the student can read. If I read the questions aloud, that would throw all the results off. I can't expect you to understand that. You haven't been trained in educational testing."

"No, I haven't. But it seems fairly obvious to me that you are not entirely objective in this matter. You are acting vindictively."

Phyllis took a menacing step toward her, her eyes narrowing to furious slits. "Let me tell you something, you little meddler. If I had my way, not only would Manuel be removed from my class, but the Gomezes would leave this ranch forever!"

"But that's ridiculous!" Leigh's voice rose in amazement. "Shane would never agree to that."

Phyllis tossed her flaming hair. "Yes, and doesn't it make you wonder why?"

"That seems simple enough. María was raised here. José has been here since their marriage. They are long-time, faithful employees. Shane would never be so ungrateful as to turn them out. No matter who pressed him to do so."

"You really are as naive as you seem, aren't you?"

Leigh was suddenly tired of Phyllis's outrageous innuendos. She was obviously hinting at something—although what it was Leigh could not even guess—and perhaps she hoped Leigh would try to drag it out of her. Then she could have the pleasure of refusing to satisfy Leigh's curiosity! But Leigh wasn't interested in taking Phyllis's bait. Seeing that Phyllis had moved to one side of the hall, Leigh hurried past her. "If you will excuse me, I'll say good night."

When she reached her apartment door, she turned, with her hand on the knob, and saw that Phyllis had followed her part of the distance. She stood now, still several steps away, but close enough for Leigh to hear the whispered words as they hissed through Phyllis's teeth.

"Manuel is Shane's son! That's why he wouldn't let the Gomezes leave here!" With that, Phyllis turned on her heel and stalked away. When she reached the door at the end of the hall, she straightened her shoulders and tossed

113

her thick hair before going outside, as if an unpleasant, but necessary, task had been completed.

For a long moment Leigh stood as if frozen, her hand on the knob, staring after Phyllis. Then she let herself into her apartment and locked the door behind her. Without bothering to turn on a light, she sank into the nearest chair. Phyllis's spiteful words echoed inside the dark living room, reverberating as if they bounced off the walls: *Manuel is Shane's son!*

Was it a lie? Phyllis clearly suspected that something was going on between Leigh and Shane; she would not hesitate to lie if she thought it would be in her own interests.

Abstractedly Leigh's fingers pulled the combs from her upswept hair, allowing it to fall heavily about her shoulders. She put her head back against the soft padding of the chair and tried to think. What was it Mary had said about Phyllis? *She fights dirty.* Leigh sighed deeply and ran trembling fingers through her hair. She realized she wanted quite desperately to believe that Phyllis had lied.

Suddenly her conversation with Rod earlier that evening took on new meaning. It was difficult now to imagine Shane Casey ever taking an interest in María. But Rod said she had been a beauty as a young girl. *All the young Mexican men in the neighborhood were after her. Even a few of the Anglos.* Had Shane been one of them?

Now she understood what Rod had meant when he remarked that she obviously had heard some of the local gossip. What Phyllis had told her was not the redhead's own private invention. It was gossip of long-standing.

It doesn't really matter whether something that was whispered about eight or nine years ago was real or only imagined, Rod had said. And Manuel was eight years old. Of course, this is what Rod had been hinting at, although he hadn't had the poor taste to come right out with it. Clearly he thought she'd already heard the tale. Or perhaps he was afraid to make such an accusation against the wealthy brother who provided his bed and board. But ever since her first day in this house, Leigh had been aware of Rod's resentment of his brother, which he tried to keep

114

buried because of his dependence on Shane. Apparently Rod had found her a good sounding board, for on more than one occasion when they were alone, he had voiced his resentment of Shane. *If you have enough money, almost anything can be forgotten.*

She could easily imagine what might have happened nine years ago. Somehow, in spite of a protective father, Shane had got the young María alone and had broken down her defenses. Certainly Leigh had enough proof of his consummate ability to do that! Probably José Gomez, who was employed on a neighboring ranch, had been one of the young Mexicans paying court to María. María had become pregnant and José had married her, possibly even knowing that she was carrying another man's child. He must have loved her very much. Did he know who Manuel's father was? Leigh had never seen him show anything but admiration and respect for his employer—so maybe he didn't know. Surely if he knew, he wouldn't want to stay here.

Phyllis's bombshell made Leigh wonder about something else too. Many of the ranch hands had large families, while José and María had only Manuel. Was there something wrong with José that made it impossible for him to father a child? If so, it was even possible that he was grateful to Manuel's father, even if he didn't know his identity, for providing him, José, with a son.

These speculations were getting her nowhere. But if Phyllis imagined that this new information about Manuel would stifle Leigh's determination to help the boy, she was very wrong. Whatever had happened nine years ago, Manuel had had no part in it. He must not be made to pay for others' mistakes.

She stirred from her musings and switched on a lamp. From the courtyard outside, she could hear some of the guests beginning to say their good-nights.

She started violently as a soft tap sounded at her door. She stepped to the door and, without opening it, called, "Who is it?"

"María, Doctor Leigh." The words were low, as if María didn't want to be overheard by others in the house.

115

Leigh swung the door open. "Come in, María."

"I can't. We still have the cleaning up to do." She glanced down the hallway rather furtively. "I just want you to know, I have talked to José. We would be grateful if you would take Manuel to San Antonio for the tests you spoke of."

What had happened, Leigh wondered, to give María this sudden burst of courage? Perhaps Phyllis had finally said too much to the woman. "I think you have made the right decision, María. I will make an appointment as soon as possible."

"We will pay for the tests." María's plump chin was held high in a proudly defiant way.

"All right. And don't let's tell anyone else about this until we get the test results."

María frowned. "I—I already spoke of it to Miss Calhoun. I didn't mean to, only she made me so angry."

"She mentioned it to me, and I suspect she thinks she's talked me out of the notion. We'll let her keep thinking that for now. Okay?"

"Yes. Now I must get back to work." María hurried toward the kitchen as Leigh closed the door.

She glanced at her watch; it was after eleven. Would Bruce still be awake in San Antonio? She decided to chance it, and when he answered with an alert voice, she was glad that she had made the call. She explained briefly about Manuel's problem and asked if he would schedule a testing session for the next Saturday.

"I'll try," he agreed. "There are several guidance centers here, and I'm sure any one of them would have the facilities for testing. Let me make some calls and get back to you."

"Thank you, Bruce."

"Is everything all right? You seem a little down. How's your social life?" The words were teasing, but Leigh had the clear impression that he was intensely interested in the answer.

"Rather dull, I'm afraid."

"I find that hard to believe."

116

"I have to go now, Bruce. Call me as soon as you have something definite on the tests."

"I will. And, listen, it shouldn't take all day. Will you stay over for a few hours and spend some time with me? I just discovered a fantastic new hamburger palace. They have more than thirty varieties."

"Of burgers?" She laughed. "Is that possible?"

"Let me prove it to you. The boy might enjoy it too."

"I'm sure he'll be delighted."

"Good, then we'll make a day of it."

She replaced the receiver and undressed slowly, thinking about Manuel and what the new tests could mean for him. What a terrible disappointment it would be if the results turned out to be the same as Phyllis's. But Leigh wouldn't allow herself to entertain the possibility. Slipping out of her underclothes, she went into the bathroom and turned on the shower.

Afterward she put on a nightgown and, taking up the novel she had been reading, she settled down on the living room couch to try to lose herself in the story. To her surprise she did get involved with the characters on the page in front of her and had read more than two chapters when she heard footsteps coming down the hall outside the apartment. The tread was heavy, but muffled by the thick carpeting. Slowly Leigh put her book face down on the couch at her side, her gaze fixed on the door.

The footsteps stopped and, as she watched with pounding heart, the doorknob turned slowly. Someone was trying to get in. Shane. Hardly allowing herself to breathe, Leigh kept her gaze fixed on the doorknob. It returned to its original position and turned once more. Then she heard the footsteps moving away. There was no other sound in the midnight silence.

She realized that her hands were gripping the edge of the upholstered cushion where she sat. And, with a dull feeling of desperation, she admitted, too, what a struggle it had been to keep from running across the room and throwing open the door. But she had done it. Maybe Shane would believe now that she would not be another of his conquests. Whatever momentary pleasures capitulation might provide, she was certain that the aftermath would not be worth the price.

She tried to return to her book, but she could no longer concentrate on imaginary conflicts; her own real-life ones kept intruding. Eventually she turned out the light and went to bed. She lay awake a long time. Somewhere in the far reaches of the house she heard a telephone ringing. The ringing stopped then, and she wondered who would be calling at such a late hour. She was certain all the guests had departed some time ago.

Through her open bedroom window she heard the droning of crickets and the distant, mournful hooting of an owl. Her eyelids had begun to grow heavy when she heard the faint crunching of gravel. Someone was walking on the drive that ran alongside her bedroom.

Then, farther away, a voice. "I'll go with you—"

"Go back into the house, Rod!" It was Shane's voice. Rod's words had apparently stopped him very near her bedroom window, for even though the words were spoken softly, she could hear them clearly. "You don't think I want you along, do you?"

Rod did not reply, and she heard the gravel crunching again as Shane walked on toward the garages. Shortly she heard the powerful motor of the Mercedes come to life, and the car backed out of the drive and sped away from the house.

Where on earth could Shane be going at this time of night? Suddenly the answer was painfully clear: to Phyllis. When Leigh had locked her door against him, he had decided to find satisfaction elsewhere. After all, one female body was much like another, wasn't it? And he had certainly made it clear tonight that it was only her body that interested him. Of course, he wouldn't want Rod along!

A hard clump of anguish throbbed in her throat. She swallowed convulsively as tears slid from beneath her closed lashes.

How she hated him!

EIGHT

"What are you up to now, Leigh?" Shane's eyes narrowed as they studied her.

To her dismay he had been having breakfast in the kitchen when she arrived there. María had brought Manuel to work with her so that Leigh could take him to San Antonio for the tests Bruce Landing had scheduled. Fortunately Manuel had been told only that he was to be allowed to go on an outing with Doctor Leigh. His excitement over the prospect was evident in his dancing brown eyes and the nervous energy he was expending by hopping from one foot to the other at Leigh's side.

"What makes you think I'm up to something?" Leigh forced her eyes wide in a look of injured innocence. "I merely thought Manuel would enjoy getting away from the ranch for the day." She glanced about to discover that María and Maggie had mysteriously disappeared, and then she heard their voices coming from the pantry, where they were evidently making a shopping list.

Unable to contain himself any longer Manuel darted for the door. "I'm going to wait in your car, Doctor Leigh."

Leigh started to follow him, but Shane's voice detained her. "Are you seeing Bruce Landing today?"

She turned to look at him. He had pushed his chair away from the table and was lighting a slim cheroot. She saw from his expression that she had not allayed his suspicions. His brazen questions annoyed her.

"Would you like me to write down my itinerary so that you'll know where I am every minute?"

He raised the cheroot to his lips and inhaled slowly,

119

watching her with a one-sided smile. "That won't be necessary. It's your day off."

"I was beginning to think you had forgotten."

"You certainly are on the defensive this morning." He held the cheroot between thumb and forefinger and studied it for a moment. "I can't help wondering why. And also, why you would want to spend your Saturday with an eight-year-old child." He took another drag on the cheroot.

Leigh brushed an imaginary speck of dust from the collar of her blue knit pantsuit. "Maybe I'm the maternal type," she retorted.

He chuckled. "It seems I learn new things about you all the time. But I think there's more to it than that."

His level gaze was beginning to unnerve her. "Is it a crime for me to take an interest in Manuel? It seems to me that someone has to. Since *you* refuse——" She bit back the words that trembled on her lips, stunned at what she had almost blurted out.

He frowned slightly, his gaze never leaving her face. "More than twenty children live on this ranch, Leigh. Are you suggesting that I ought to single out Manuel for special privileges? What are you getting at anyway?"

His seeming lack of interest in the child who, according to Phyllis Calhoun, was his own son, angered Leigh. "Well, if *you* don't know, I can't tell you."

With sudden alertness he sat forward in his chair, his hands braced on his knees, smoke filtering from the cheroot held between the fingers of one hand. The gray eyes were bright. "If you have something to say, say it."

She felt a pulse beating furiously in her throat as she took a step backward toward the door. "You are the one who started this conversation, not I."

After a moment he settled back into a more relaxed position and tapped the ash from his cheroot into his saucer. "I have asked several perfectly civil questions and have received no answers, only evasions."

"Did it ever occur to you that I might resent being quizzed by my employer about how I spend my time off?"

120

"I don't know why that should be, unless you have something to hide."

"W-well," she stammered, "it's the principle involved." A flush had risen to her cheeks.

"I see." His wide lips curved into a teasing smile. "So you *are* seeing Landing today."

"I didn't say——"

"You don't have to." He rested one booted foot on his other knee and tipped the chair back on two legs. "I think I know why you're taking Manuel now."

Could he possibly? Worriedly her eyes scanned his face, taking in the mocking expression. Would he try to stop her? Well, he couldn't! She would defy him if she had to, although the prospect sent a shivery sensation down her spine. Unconsciously she squared her shoulders, as if she were preparing to do battle.

"You have been thinking over what I said about Landing," he drawled. "You've realized that his interest in you goes deeper than friendship. So you are taking Manuel as a sort of chaperon."

"That's absurd!"

"Is it?" There was a wicked gleam in his eyes. "I fully expect to discover next that you've taken Manuel to live with you. Will he sleep on your living room couch? The edge of sarcasm told her this was an oblique reference to the night he had come to her apartment at midnight and tried the door. Did he know she'd been sitting on the other side, watching the knob turn? But he couldn't know. He was only guessing.

"I hardly think José and María would agree to that."

"What a shame." The tone was studiously grave now. "You will have to continue to fend for yourself."

His arrogance made her temper rise again. It was difficult to reply calmly. "Which I will do as often and as long as is necessary." Her violet-blue eyes blazed at him now. "*No one* is irresistible."

He held her gaze for a long moment. Then he said in a soft, deliberate way, "If I ever make up my mind to seduce you, Leigh, I don't think you will offer too much resistance."

"Why, you—" She went rigid with indignation, her small hands curled into fists at her sides.

He laughed. "The truth is often hard to accept, isn't it?"

"You are insufferable! You are—" She heard a gasp behind her and turned to see Maggie and María at the pantry door. They were staring at her as if she'd lost her mind.

"Excuse me." She gulped as she turned on her heel and left the kitchen. What would Shane say to them? How would he explain her anger? It might be interesting to watch him try, she thought grimly. But then, he wasn't in the habit of explaining anything to servants. He would probably walk out of the kitchen and leave the two women to draw their own conclusions. Maggie and María would probably expect him to fire her after that outburst. Somehow Leigh knew that Shane wouldn't do that. He enjoyed having her around to taunt too much. As she walked along the gravel drive toward the garages, she thought that it might make things simpler all around if he did dismiss her. Or if she resigned. But she wouldn't do that either. She wanted to keep this job. She loved the ranch and the horses. Besides, she wouldn't give Shane the pleasure of hearing her admit defeat.

During the drive to San Antonio she told Manuel that he would be spending the morning taking tests. His round little face fell at this information. "I do not like tests, señorita. Miss Calhoun gives me many tests, and always I do not do well."

Leigh patted his head. "Miss Calhoun has nothing to do with these tests. Just do your best, and then we will have hamburgers with Doctor Landing."

His brown forehead creased worriedly. "You mean it doesn't matter how these tests turn out?"

"You don't have to worry about that," Leigh told him, hoping that his obvious anxiety over the tests was not going to affect the outcome. She had an inspiration. "Nobody knows that you are being tested today except your parents and me. Afterward we will talk and decide if we want to tell anybody else. *You* can decide."

"Oh." He looked up at her with a puzzled little grin. "And then we will have hamburgers?"

She laughed. "Scout's honor. French fries and a malt, too, if you want."

The brown eyes cleared instantly. He settled back against the seat, grinning. Then he said, "What is this 'scout's honor'?"

"Oh, that's just an expression, Manuel. Have you heard of the Boy Scouts? When a scout gives his word on something, then he has to do what he says or break the Boy Scout oath. So when I said, 'Scout's honor,' it was like saying, 'Cross my heart' or, 'What I'm saying is the truth.' "

Manuel was thoughtful for a moment. "It is like when my father says, 'By the Virgin'?"

"Something like that, Manuel."

They met Bruce at the guidance center. The psychologist who would be administering the tests was male, a fact which Leigh hoped would help to put Manuel at ease. The bearded, young Dr. David Bumgarten wore faded jeans and a knit shirt with TODAY IS THE FIRST DAY OF THE REST OF YOUR LIFE printed in psychedelic letters across the front. In manner and appearance, he was as far removed from Phyllis Calhoun as it was possible to be. Within minutes Manuel was chatting easily with him.

When Dr. Bumgarten felt that Manuel was sufficiently comfortable with him, he said to Leigh, "Doctor Landing has explained the situation to me. The tests will take about two hours. You can wait here in the waiting room or leave and come back about eleven."

Manuel cast an uneasy glance in Leigh's direction. "You will be here when I'm finished, won't you?"

Leigh gave him a reassuring smile. "Yes. We'll probably go out for coffee, but we'll be back soon."

"Okay," Manuel agreed and went readily into the testing room with the psychologist.

They took Bruce's car and found a restaurant close to the center. After they were settled in a corner booth and had ordered coffee, Leigh said, "You did tell Doctor Bumgarten about the language problem, didn't you?"

"Relax. They're equipped to handle things like that."

Leigh did relax. "Good." She sipped her steaming coffee. "It's kind of you to arrange this for Manuel."

"I had a selfish motive. I wanted to see you."

His thoughtful gaze made her feel a little uncomfortable. She smiled uncertainly, and he went on. "Manuel's a charmer, isn't he?"

Leigh nodded. "But his teacher is determined to put him in a learning-disabled class."

"Do you think you can stop her?"

"If these tests prove I'm right," she said grimly, "I'm going to do my darndest. I'll take the results to the school board."

"Manuel's parents work for Shane Casey, didn't you say? It might be a good idea to get him to speak for Manuel to the board. He surely has a lot of influence in this part of the state."

"Shane's a member of the board," Leigh told him. "He's one of the people I have to convince."

"Oh." Bruce's shoulders lifted in an offhand gesture. "He certainly seems to be a reasonable man."

"Reasonable!"

Bruce regarded her gravely. "I haven't wanted to say anything, but you seem tired, Leigh. On edge, or preoccupied about something. Is your job not working out as you had hoped?"

"The job is fine."

"Then have you had a run-in with Shane Casey?"

"I don't know what you mean by a run-in, Bruce. He hasn't criticized my work, if that's what you mean." She sighed and gazed out the glass beside the booth. Cars passed on a busy San Antonio street. "But he is arrogant and conceited and—cruel."

When she looked back at Bruce, he was staring at her in amazement. "I find that hard to believe. When we had dinner, he seemed so congenial."

"Oh, he can lay on the charm when it suits him."

"Can he?" The hazel eyes had turned speculative. "Well, he surely seems to have rubbed you the wrong way."

"That's putting it mildly," she retorted. "He's been nothing but trouble since the day I arrived at the ranch. I can't stand the man."

Bruce did not speak for a moment. "If the conditions are so unpleasant, why don't you quit?"

"What?" She blinked in surprise. "And let him have the last laugh? Never!"

He smiled ruefully. "Then you don't really want to leave."

"I—why, no. I love the horses, and—"

"You're not quite as certain about your feelings for Shane Casey as you pretend."

Flustered, she toyed with a salt shaker. "I don't know what you mean."

He laid a big hand over her fidgeting fingers. "I mean that hate and love are sometimes two sides of the same emotion."

"Oh, Bruce, I've never believed that old wives' tale."

"A lot of old wives' tales have some basis in fact. If you didn't feel something for the man, he couldn't make you so angry."

She squirmed on the plastic seat. "Will you stop looking at me like that? Go ahead and say it."

"Say what?"

"Whatever it is you're thinking."

He shrugged. "I was only thinking that Shane Casey is a lucky man."

She forced a laugh. "Can't we talk about something besides Shane Casey?"

He patted her hand and let it go. "Sure. But that won't keep you from thinking about him, will it?" He held up a hand. "Okay. I'll shut up. What do you think Manuel would enjoy doing after lunch?"

Leigh relaxed as they planned the day, deciding to visit the Lone Star Brewery's famous Buckhorn Hall of Horns later in the afternoon and, after that, the Mexican Market if there was time. They idled over a second cup of coffee and returned to the guidance center. They had been in the waiting room for a half hour when Dr. Bumgarten appeared.

"Manuel will be out in a minute."

"How—how did the tests turn out?" Leigh asked anxiously.

David Bumgarten smiled and tugged at his beard. "I still have some tabulating to do, but I'm sure of one thing. Manuel isn't retarded." Leigh let out a long breath of relief. "In fact," Dr. Bumgarten went on, "his intelligence is probably above average. I'll have the secretary type a detailed description of the tests I gave him along with the results and my recommendations. I'll mail those to you."

"What about the reading problem?"

"As you suspected, Manuel has been a little confused by having to switch back and forth from Spanish to English. He does need some special help with reading. Once he reaches his grade level, though, I don't expect him to have any more trouble. Manuel's situation is far from unique, I'm afraid. The standardized tests used in American schools assume verbal ability in English. For children who come from culturally deprived backgrounds or from homes where a foreign language is spoken, this works against them. The tests can't accurately measure intelligence or aptitude in such children. I am surprised Manuel's teacher didn't take that into consideration."

"I can't thank you enough for taking Manuel on Saturday like this," Leigh said. "The school board meets a week from Monday. I'll need the test results by then."

"You will have them," Dr. Bumgarten assured her. "Ah, here is our young man now. He tells me he's going to have a hamburger and a strawberry malt for lunch."

"*A* hamburger," Bruce said, cocking his head in mock consternation. "I thought surely he could eat at least two."

Manuel grinned broadly. "I will try, señor."

Dr. Bumgarten and Manuel took leave of each other like two old friends. Outside, Bruce suggested Leigh leave her car there to be picked up before she and Manuel left for the ranch.

"Doctor David is a nice man," Manuel told them as they got into Bruce's car. "I think he liked me."

"*Amigo*," Leigh said, "how could he help it?" and Manuel laughed happily.

The remainder of the day passed quickly. Manuel's eyes

126

grew wider and he became more animated with each new sight. At the Buckhorn Hall of Horns he was so enthralled by the stuffed animals and mounted horns and antlers— not to mention all the free root beer he could drink—that they stayed later than planned. As they left the hall it was growing dark and Bruce took them back to the guidance center, where he transferred a drowsy Manuel to Leigh's Volkswagen. Leigh got behind the wheel and, after thanking Bruce again for the day, left the city, a sleeping Manuel curled in the seat beside her.

As the houses on the outskirts of San Antonio dwindled, she glanced again and again at the sleeping child. She couldn't wait to tell María and José the results of the tests. She felt certain they would be awake and waiting anxiously for Manuel's return.

Her scrutiny rested on Manuel's small, straight nose, the black brows and long lashes, the round little chin. Was there anything of Shane Casey in that face? The chin and the eyes were María's. But other than that, he was simply Manuel. She could see nothing of Shane in him. But, she thought wistfully, that might be because she didn't want to.

When she arrived at the Gomez house, she found only María there to listen to her recital. Although obviously still concerned about challenging Phyllis Calhoun's recommendations, María was thrilled by Leigh's summation of Dr. Bumgarten's words and agreed to go to the school board meeting with Leigh.

"Where is José?" Leigh asked finally.

"Still at the barn. One of the mares is trying to have her colt, and she is having some trouble."

The roan, Leigh thought. "Wouldn't you know she'd go into labor while I was gone?"

She hurried back to her car, thinking, Why didn't we come home right after the tests? But Manuel would have been so disappointed. She drove as fast as she dared over the narrow graveled lane and soon saw the lighted barn ahead. She pulled up beside the door, jumped out, and ran inside.

One of the stall doors was standing open. José and

Shane were just inside the stall, looking worriedly and rather helplessly at the mare, who lay prone on a bed of hay. Both of the men appeared rumpled and weary, as if they had been keeping their vigil for some time.

Shane turned as Leigh entered the stall. "Thank God you're here."

"This was the wrong day to leave the ranch," she said grimly.

"You couldn't have known, and we thought it was going to be a normal delivery until the last hour or so." Shane's tired eyes raked over her knit pantsuit. "You'd better go change clothes before examining her."

"I think I saw a pair of coveralls in the office." She found the coveralls folded on top of an old file cabinet and, stepping into them quickly, tugged at the zipper. They must belong to José or another of the hired men. They were too small for Shane, although still much too large for her. She found a pair of rubber gloves and returned to the stall.

The mare was exhausted. The examination was accomplished quickly. This is one situation, Leigh thought, when a woman's smaller hands and arms are an advantage.

When she had finished the examination, she stripped off the gloves. José was bending over the mare, talking soothingly to her.

"The foal is turned sideways," she said to Shane. "We may have to pull it, but we'll try injections first. We have that new medication. I doubt that you've used it before. There wasn't any here when I came, and it's relatively new on the market."

"How long before we know whether she can deliver on her own?" Shane's concern was understandable. If the foal had to be taken, there was always the possibility of damage to either or both the mare and her baby.

"Two or three hours." Leigh went to the supply cabinet and found the medication she wanted. Shane followed her, leaning tiredly against the cabinet while they waited for the water to boil for sterilizing the syringe.

After a moment he said, "There's room for two of you in those coveralls."

She shrugged uninterestedly. "Plenty of space to move around."

She checked her watch. The water had been boiling long enough. She removed the syringe with tongs and laid it on a sterile towel to cool.

"You're the only woman I know," Shane said unexpectedly, "who could look feminine in such an outrageous getup."

She glanced at him. The soft eyes were admiring and without rancor. She returned his smile. "I could use a cup of coffee. How about you?"

"Several," he agreed. "We're going to be here awhile."

When she got the coffeepot from the cabinet, he took it out of her hands. "I'll do that. You take care of the mare."

While she administered the injection, Shane made the coffee and brought three chairs from the barn office, setting them near the mare's stall. The sympathetic José wanted to remain in the stall, however, so Shane carried his coffee to him. The Mexican man's thoughts were entirely on the suffering roan. He made no reference to Leigh's trip to San Antonio. As for Leigh, she much preferred that José hear the story from María. She didn't want to discuss the reason for her trip in front of Shane.

Shane settled down on one of the chairs beside Leigh. "I hope we can save this one," he said. "There are excellent bloodlines on both sides."

"I'm going to do everything in my power to save it," Leigh said.

He reached out to lay his strong fingers over the hand that rested on her thigh. "I know you are."

"I imagine you've spent a number of nights like this," she said, moving restlessly. He removed his hand without comment and nodded. She slid down into the chair so that her head rested against the padded back. She unzipped the front of the coveralls because it was a little stuffy in the barn, even though the loft fan was on and stirring the air. A nervous whinny from Lady, who was spending the night in a stall on the other end of the barn, caused Leigh to stir.

"She's restless," Shane said. "She knows something's going on."

After that, the labored breathing of the roan was the only other sound in the barn for some time. Leigh began to find herself drifting into sleep, the warm slumberous night invading her. It seemed that she had only just slipped into a light doze when a strong hand stroked down the curve of her cheek, lingering on the soft skin. She slowly opened her eyes, feeling, in the moment before her defenses came up, a languorous spread of pleasure as she looked into Shane's dark face.

"You said you wanted to check the mare every twenty minutes."

She sat up, yawning. "Sorry. I didn't mean to fall asleep."

"You're tired. You've had a long day."

She said offhandedly, "I'll sleep tomorrow."

After examining the roan, she came out of the stall. Shane was at the hot plate making another pot of coffee.

"She's having some contractions now," Leigh said. "It's going to be a while, though. I tried to get José to come out of the stall. He refused, naturally."

"Naturally."

"At least, he's resting on some bales of hay. He's totally devoted to the horses, isn't he?"

Shane refilled their coffee mugs and handed one to her. "Yes. I'm fortunate to have him. José and I have been through a lot together."

Leigh watched him as he sipped the coffee, wondering if there were hidden meanings in his remark. He caught her gaze with a questioning look, and she glanced away. They returned to their chairs. "Go back to sleep if you can," Shane said. "I'll wake you if anything happens."

After finishing her coffee, she found a comfortable position and closed her eyes, but she didn't sleep. She listened to the mare's heavy breathing and, farther away, the soft night sounds. The silence was comfortable, making her feel an easy companionship with the man beside her. At the moment they were both too concerned about the mare to think about other things. As the minutes passed, Leigh

130

felt a silent communication with the two men who kept the vigil with her that she had not felt before. Shane's presence was especially supportive. Some employers would have gone to bed and left her and José to cope with the mare. She was sure the idea had not even occurred to Shane.

A little after two, the mare delivered a skinny, but large-framed, foal with only a little help from Leigh.

"Doctor Leigh, you have done it!" José beamed at the scrawny, roan-colored foal, who was already trying to stand. "Look at him! Already he wants to run."

Leigh smiled happily, wiping at the perspiration on her forehead with the back of her hand. Shane, who had been at her side during the delivery, put his arm around her, pulling her against his side. "Good work, Doctor." He smiled down at her.

It felt right somehow to have Shane's arm around her at that moment of shared accomplishment, and she didn't try to pull away. The colt was still struggling to stand while the mare lifted her head and whinnied worriedly.

"Go home and rest, José," Shane said. "We've done all we can do for now."

José stretched wearily, but he still seemed reluctant to leave until Shane insisted. When the Mexican man was gone, Shane's arm dropped from Leigh's shoulders and he walked over to the colt who had, at last, gotten his wobbly legs beneath him. Shane looked down at the foal, frowning.

Leigh moved to his side. "What's wrong?"

He pointed. "Take a good look at his legs."

On closer scrutiny, Leigh saw what he meant. The colt's front legs had an abnormal bending at the knees, so that the legs bowed out slightly. Horsemen called the abnormality bench-knees. Leigh knew the condition was related to a growth plate just above the knee—scientifically, the proximal radial epiphysis. It was the area that was radiographed to determine when a horse was ready to race. In the young horse the disk was sandwiched between two large pieces of bone and, until he was about two years of age, it continually produced an even layer of bone on each surface, causing the legs to lengthen. Evidently something had happened while this colt was in the womb that caused more growth on the outside of the front limbs than on the inside, producing the bowed-out effect.

"I don't like the looks of that at all," Shane said.

He looked so disappointed that Leigh felt an urge to comfort him. "Let's give him a few hours to get steadier on his legs. It's a little too early to make a diagnosis."

"All right," he said with a disheartened expression, "but I don't think it's going to make any difference. You're right about one thing. We need some rest."

Leigh took off the coveralls and returned them to the office. Then they walked back to the house together in silence. After a quick shower Leigh fell into a restless sleep. Her dreams were filled with delivering foals, one after the other, all dead. Finally, at six thirty, she got up and ate a breakfast of scrambled eggs and toast. She was back at the barn by seven. As early as it was, however, Shane was there before her. He had, she saw, shaved and changed to clean jeans and shirt, but when she saw the tired lines around his eyes, she doubted that he had slept at all.

He was just taking a fresh pot of coffee from the hot plate. "Why do I have the feeling I've seen this all before?" Leigh said.

He turned to her with an accusatory look. "You're supposed to be resting."

"I also have the feeling that you tricked me into going to bed and then came right back here."

He grinned. "I didn't. I slept for a while."

"How long?"

"About as long as you did, I'll wager." He lifted his mug to her. "Want a cup?"

"No, I just had one." She walked toward the mare's stall. "How does he look this morning?"

"I don't want to prejudice you," Shane said, setting down his cup and following her to the stall.

She looked at the colt, who was nursing now, for a long moment. Then she glanced at Shane. "It didn't magically disappear overnight, did it?"

"Afraid not." He seemed to be taking the abnormality philosophically this morning. "I haven't seen the condition many times, but often enough to know one thing: That horse will never race."

She stood, hands on hips, watching the colt nudge his mother with his nose. "I'm surprised at you, Shane. I didn't think you'd give up without a fight."

His eyebrows lifted. "I know when to accept the inevitable."

"What makes you think this is inevitable?"

"It would take a miracle to correct those legs."

"Okay," she said brightly. "Let's try for a miracle."

"Are we going to have a prayer meeting, or what?"

"No, we're going to cast those legs."

He was silent for a moment, staring at her. "Are you sure? I mean, have you ever done it before?"

"I've seen it done several times. It's the best hope we have, so what do we have to lose?"

After another moment of seeming uncertainty he grinned. "Now I know why you had all that casting material on the list you gave me. Do you know I almost didn't buy it?"

"A good thing you decided to indulge me, though I didn't think we'd need it quite so soon. You'll have to help me. This is one job for which I freely admit I'm not strong enough alone."

He made a mock bow. "Tell me what to do, Doctor."

They had to separate the colt from his mother while they worked. About an hour later they carried the colt with his two stiffly casted front legs back to his mother, who sniffed the casts thoroughly, then nuzzled her baby's neck. As for the colt, his front legs were awkward, but with help he learned to stand on them. Leigh and Shane laughed as they watched his attempts to walk.

At last Leigh said, "We'll know in a few weeks if it's going to work. If it doesn't, there's the more drastic treatment of putting surgical staples across the outside of the knees until the growth on the inside catches up."

Shane was studying her with an admiring gleam in his gray eyes. "As I said before, you're a stubborn lady."

Leigh realized that this time he obviously meant it as a compliment. "If I recall our first meeting correctly, you said I'd need to be to work for you."

He grinned. "Did I say that?"

"You certainly did. More stubborn than your horses is, I believe, the way you put it."

He frowned, watching her. "I've been pretty hard on you, haven't I?"

She looked away, flushing. "Once or twice." He put a hand under her chin and turned her head toward him.

She lifted her lashes to look into his face. All at once her heart was beating very fast. The gray eyes stared into her own and then dropped to her soft mouth. Slowly Shane lowered his head toward her just as her head moved up to meet him. Their mouths met in a sensuous joining that she felt in every cell of her body.

She had not known, until the moment of their touching, that she wanted him to kiss her. She had only felt a yearning sort of sweetness stirring to life inside her. Now she opened her lips under his, returning his kiss, which was as sweet as honey and as deep as forever, and her hands moved up his arms to his shoulders and onto his neck to cling there, her fingers pressing into his strong, warm flesh. She had the strange sensation that if she did not hang on to him, she would fall from a precipice.

His hands enclosed her body, lifting and pressing her against him. She began to feel a dreamy unreality creeping over her, a swooning almost, as if the fire of his kiss was melting her.

His mouth explored her cheeks and her throat, while his hands slid down her body and pressed against the soft curves of her hips. She had never known such blinding desire. She was trembling with it, wanting to touch him everywhere, to explore every inch of his long, lean body. One of his hands had moved to the front of her blouse, where the fingers traced the outline of her breast through the thin cotton of her clothing, causing her to moan and push against his hand. Her heart raced under his touch.

"Leigh," he said hoarsely. He lifted his face to look into her eyes. He looked dazed for a moment and then some-

134

thing—some stab of pain or regret—twisted his mouth. "You must go," he said harshly, putting her away from him.

Leigh stood there, staring at him blindly for a moment. Why was he pushing her out of his arms? He had been as lost in desire as she. She turned away, her hand feeling, like a sightless person's, for the outer wooden wall of the stall. Had he only wanted to prove what he'd told her the morning before—that he could seduce her if he tried?

Reality was coming back now—painfully. The overwhelming rush of sensual pleasure, so wondrously new to her, was not new to him. Perhaps it became less overpowering, the more one experienced it. It did not seem possible, certainly, that such explosive feelings could be repeated indefinitely. Yet even as she told herself this, she did not believe it. She knew Shane would always be able to arouse such feelings in her. It was only fortunate that he'd decided to stop himself when she'd lost all semblance of sense or reason.

"Leigh. . . ." Suddenly she felt his hands on her shoulders. He was standing behind her, his fingers digging painfully into the flesh. She stood still, her head bowed, and felt the warmth of his breath in her hair.

His fingers relaxed then. "Go, get some rest." His voice sounded muffled and strange, and his hands dropped away.

She nodded without looking back at him and left the barn, feeling more confused than ever. By the time she had reached her apartment, she was hot with shame. What a fool she was! It was not as if she could not have any other man. Bruce Landing would like to marry her; she knew that, even though he had never put it into words. It was possible that Rod might also, given a little encouragement. But she had nothing to give to Bruce or Rod except friendship. The rest of her, body and soul, longed for the strength, the arrogance of Shane Casey—a man capable of going from her arms to Phyllis Calhoun's, all in a few minutes' time, without a twinge of conscience. A man who lorded it over his own brother and denied his illegitimate son.

She wanted to hate him, but all she felt when he had

her in his arms was a hopeless longing . . . love. Yes, it had to be love that she felt for Shane. Nothing else could be so overpowering, nor so fraught with despair. She should leave the ranch without further delay, leave and never lay eyes on Shane Casey again. If she had any sense . . . but hadn't she just proved that she had very little of that?

NINE

Leigh backed the Volkswagen out of the garage, turned, and drove away from the house. She had waited until Shane was gone before leaving for the school-board meeting in order to avoid having to answer his questions. What would he think when he saw her walk in with María?

María sat beside her, dressed in a black skirt and white tailored blouse; she was twisting a lace-edged handkerchief nervously between her fingers.

"Are you sure what I'm wearing is all right?" she asked Leigh for the third time in the last five minutes.

"You look fine," Leigh assured her.

María cast a timid look at her. "You will do the talking?"

Leigh smiled. "I've already said I would."

"Oh, did you bring the papers Doctor Bumgarten sent?"

Leigh patted her shoulder bag, which rested on the raised floorboard between them. "Right here in my purse."

"Do you think they will understand that José had work to do? They won't think he doesn't care what happens to his son, will they?"

"I'm sure they won't. Besides, Shane is the chairman of the board. He knows where José is. We will explain that I am speaking for both you and your husband. What's important is what is in Doctor Bumgarten's report."

María drew a long, tremulous breath. "I am sure you are right. José did not really want to come. He does not like disagreements. I do not like them either, but sometimes they are necessary. I am so happy to know that my son has a good mind."

"Did you ever really doubt it?"

137

María smiled briefly. "No, but a mother cannot always see the truth about her children. José tells me I worry too much about Manuel. I know he is right. It might not be so if I had other children—but that can never be. When Manuel was born, something inside me tore."

Leigh cast a sympathetic glance at María's troubled face. "Oh, María, I'm sorry. I didn't know that." So it wasn't José's fault that he and María had no other children. It was something she hadn't thought of, but it didn't prove that José was Manuel's father, either.

"With Mexican families, children are very important. It is a great sorrow for José and me that we can't have any more babies."

"I'm sure it must be," Leigh commiserated. "Perhaps Manuel will give you many grandchildren one day."

A soft smile touched María's lips. "I have often dreamed of that day."

They had left the ranch and were approaching San Lorenzo. "María," Leigh said, "I think you should be prepared for what might happen tonight. Phyllis Calhoun is not going to like being challenged at a public meeting."

María looked at her sharply. "You don't have to warn me, Doctor Leigh. I have felt the sting of that woman's sharp tongue many times. As long as Manuel is not put into that special class where he doesn't belong, she can say nothing that will hurt me."

"Good." But Leigh wasn't so sure. What if Phyllis lost her head and blurted out something about Manuel's father? She forced this troublesome thought aside. Surely even Phyllis could not be that cruel. She turned off the highway into a paved parking area next to the brick school building and found an empty spot not far from the entrance. She looked at María. "Ready to brave the lioness in her den?"

María laughed nervously. "We will trim her claws tonight, eh?"

"Right to the quick," Leigh returned. They walked toward the lighted school building and, as they reached the glass double-doors at the entrance, Leigh gripped her shoulder bag, containing the psychologist's report, to her side. Thinking about what the report contained bolstered her confidence.

The meeting was to be held in the superintendent's office. When Leigh and María entered, Shane was sitting with four other men on one side of a long table, their backs to the wall. Folding chairs had been set up on the other side of the room in two rows. Several people were already seated, including Phyllis, who looked up as Leigh and María entered, her tawny eyes sweeping over the two women before she tossed her head and looked away.

Leigh led the way to two places on the near end of the back row of folding chairs. After sitting down, she glanced toward the long table across the room. Shane was looking at her with a quizzical lift of his eyebrows.

The meeting began with a discussion of bids for the purchase of a new school bus and progressed to a debate about the hiring of a lunchroom supervisor for the next school term. It was over an hour before the matter of student transfers came up.

At this point Shane said, "We now have a very serious matter before the board—the matter of the transfer of a third-grade student, Manuel Gomez, into the learning-disabled class. Miss Calhoun, Manuel's teacher, has submitted test scores and a report on her personal observations. I believe you all have copies of these, gentlemen. Would any of you like to question Miss Calhoun about anything in her report?"

There were no questions. Evidently Phyllis's report was detailed and the conclusions based on her test scores inescapable.

"There being no questions," Shane went on, "I will allow comments from other interested parties. Manuel's mother is here tonight. María, do you wish to address the board?"

"I have brought Doctor Alexander to speak for me and my husband," María said in a clear, if somewhat shaky voice.

As Leigh extracted Dr. Bumgarten's report from her purse and stood, she felt every eye in the room resting on her. "It was the wish of Manuel's parents that Manuel be tested by an independent educational psychologist. I took him to Doctor David Bumgarten, a highly regarded specialist in aptitude and intelligence testing. I have his report here and I would like to submit it to the board."

A low murmur of several voices met this statement. As Leigh stepped forward to hand the report to Shane she caught Phyllis's rigidly angry face from the corner of her eye.

Shane gave her a disconcerted look before unfolding the report and starting to read silently. Leigh returned to her seat beside María. There was a long silence.

At last Shane cleared his throat. "Doctor Bumgarten's conclusions do not agree with Miss Calhoun's." There was a sharp intake of breath from Phyllis.

"Doctor Bumgarten's tests," Shane went on, his eyes steady on Leigh's face, "show Manuel Gomez to have an intelligence quotient of one hundred and twenty-six and a high aptitude in mechanical and mathematical areas. It is Doctor Bumgarten's conclusion that Manuel is an underachiever in the area of reading because of a home environment where Spanish is the predominant language used. He recommends that Manuel receive tutoring in reading and be placed in the fourth-grade class next term." His tone was businesslike, even cold, but there was a flame deep in the gray eyes as they stared at Leigh—a flame of anger.

Phyllis, who had been squirming in her seat, now leaped to her feet and burst out, "Lies! I don't know how she managed it, but—"

Shane snatched up a gavel resting on the table in front of him and banged it loudly. "I must ask you to remain calm, Miss Calhoun."

"But he's saying I falsified my test results!"

"He is saying nothing of the kind," Shane said sharply. "If you will allow me to finish. Doctor Bumgarten suggests that the tests you gave assumed a verbal ability in English that Manuel does not have. Therefore the results of your tests cannot be valid."

"I demand—"

"Sit down, Miss Calhoun!" Shane's deep voice vibrated

in the tensely silent room. Phyllis hesitated for a brief moment, then obeyed.

"Now, gentlemen," Shane went on in the same cold, businesslike tone with which he had summarized the psychologist's report, "does anyone care to question Doctor Bumgarten's findings?"

No one did. "Very well. We shall now vote on the matter of Manuel Gomez's transfer to a learning-disabled class. All those in favor of such a transfer, let it be known by raising their right hands." The men at the table kept their eyes lowered, but no hands went up. "Manuel Gomez is, therefore, to be enrolled in the regular fourth-grade class for the coming school year. Is there any other business?"

María was gripping Leigh's hand now, her relief and happiness apparent in the glow of her brown eyes.

"This meeting is now adjourned." Shane stood and gathered a stack of papers, stuffing them into a slim leather attaché case. The other board members left quickly, perhaps wishing to avoid conversation with Phyllis. The few spectators began leaving too.

María turned to Leigh. "Thank you! You did this for my Manuel. You are so good."

"Don't you mean conniving?" Phyllis Calhoun stood between Leigh and María and the door. Sparks shot from her almond-shaped eyes. "I don't know what you hope to gain by this underhanded little maneuver, Leigh!"

"Justice, Phyllis," Leigh replied calmly.

"My goodness, how noble!" Phyllis's laugh was shrill.

Shane had suddenly appeared at Phyllis's side. "I would like to speak to you, Phyllis. Now." The gray eyes were riveted on Leigh's face, glinting like two balls of white-hot steel. He took Phyllis's arm and, ignoring her protests, led her determinedly out of the office.

María's mouth drew together in consternation. "She does not like having her claws cut, does she?"

"No," Leigh agreed, still smarting from Shane's quelling look. "But then we expected that. Let's go home, María."

They left the school building and drove back to the ranch. After dropping María at her house, Leigh went to her apartment in a state of nervous anticipation. She was certain she had not heard the last from Shane concerning her part in the meeting tonight. He had been furious with her, and Shane Casey was not a man who smoldered in silence for very long. She made tea and carried a cup into the living room. She had not long to wait. She'd had only a few sips when there was a loud banging at her door. "Let me in, Leigh!"

"It's late," she returned in a voice that was unsteady.

"Open this door before I break it down!"

Good Lord, he would bring Maggie and Rod running. It was even possible that his thundering commands could be heard as faraway as the workers' houses. What right did he have to humiliate her like this? She strode across the room and threw open the door.

Shane brushed past her rudely, slamming the door behind him. He stood with his back to the door. "I have come for an explanation," he barked.

"I thought I made everything perfectly clear at the board meeting," she flung at him. "Phyllis tried to railroad Manuel into another class. Doctor Bumgarten was being kind when he suggested in his report that her decision was based merely on wrong assumptions. I think she knew exactly what she was doing."

"Whether she did or not is immaterial at the moment." Shane moved away from the door and began to cross the room toward her. He looked taller than ever in his dark brown suit, and there seemed to be menace in the steely gleam in his eyes.

"Immaterial! How easily you excuse the inexcusable!"

"Don't try to divert me." He loomed above her and there was no mistaking the fury in every line and bone of him. "You handled this whole thing as if some deep, dark conspiracy were afoot. Sneaking off to San Antonio with Manuel, swearing María and José to secrecy. You deliberately kept me in the dark about it until you could drop your bombshell at the meeting tonight. Don't bother denying it."

"I have no intention of doing so!" She was as angry as he now. His pride had been hurt; that was really what was behind his outrage. "Everything I did was in Manuel's best interests. I had to make sure that he got a fair hearing tonight."

"Don't speak to me of fair!" His finely sculptured lips thinned grimly on the words. "It was anything but fair that I—your employer and the chairman of the board— was not told about those tests and the psychologist's report before the meeting." He paused and made a savage gesture toward Leigh. "You wanted me to walk into that meeting unprepared. I resent the implications of that. Did you think I'd lose my temper, throw things?"

Leigh could only look at him for a moment and wonder if his anger was for himself or Phyllis. "Do you really want to know what I expected?"

"I have said so. That is why I'm here."

"I thought you would go straight to Phyllis and that she would manage to do something to cancel out the effects of Dr. Bumgarten's report."

"And that I would aid and abet her, I suppose." His jaws tightened.

She backed away from him a few steps. "Oh, Shane, I couldn't be sure—" She sat down suddenly on the couch and looked away from him toward the closed door. She wanted desperately for him to go.

Hands gripped her shoulders—hard, relentless, pulling her to her feet and giving her a shake. "There is more to this than you have said. Phyllis swore to me that she believed her tests to be accurate. Why are you so sure she meant deliberate harm to Manuel?"

Leigh wished she could have flung Phyllis's accusation in his face, but when Shane touched her—no matter how much she despised his arrogance and cruelty—it was as if nothing mattered but the hard, warm maleness of him. She felt a deep shock along every nerve in her body, and it caused her to despise herself as much as Shane.

She straightened, trying to fight the frightening, boneless feeling that was creeping over her. "Let me go," she whispered.

He pushed her away from him so abruptly that she fell back onto the couch, her hair flying out, a swath of golden silk against the dark green of the upholstery. Shane stared down at her with narrowed, burning eyes.

"You will answer me," he growled.

"Or what?" she said, her voice breaking. "You'll hit me?"

"You told me earlier"—he seemed to be fighting for control—"that Phyllis had it in for Manuel. I want to know why."

She bit her lower lip to keep it from trembling. "Is it really necessary for me to put it into words?"

Suddenly he bent over her, his weight supported on one knee, which rested on the cushion beside her, his hands braced against the back of the couch on either side of her head. "Stop talking in riddles," he ordered.

She forced herself to meet the glowering eyes so near her own. "Phyllis told me. Did you think she was more discreet than that?" She laughed—a short, broken sound in the charged atmosphere of the apartment. "Well, if you thought that, you don't know her very well." Her violet eyes, dark with confused emotions, challenged him. "Perhaps sleeping with a woman doesn't ensure—"

"Your jealousy of Phyllis is eating you alive, isn't it?" His teeth were gritted, white and hard. "I knew the first time I saw you that you weren't the frigid career woman you pretended. How does it feel to suffer from the baser emotions like everyone else, Leigh?"

She was unable to control her sudden fury, and her hand flew up to slap his face. But he was quick as a wild animal, and both her hands were gripped and held back against the couch while his triumphant face came closer to her own. Her cry of denial was cut off as he kissed her bruisingly, forcing her down beneath him along the length of the couch. She thrashed about in an effort to free herself, but it was an uneven battle, and she was shockingly aware of his relentless weight pressing down upon her. Her fingers wrenched briefly at his hair, but as the kiss continued her grip weakened and slid down his neck, and her lips opened against her will. As her struggles ceased, his mouth eased some of its bruising force and he drew from her lips a soft groan as his mouth explored and tantalized and made her feel as if he were drawing her very soul from her body.

Then, abruptly, he lifted his weight from her body, smiling down at her in mocking triumph. She gave a stifled cry, and her hands flew up to cover her face. She despised him for his perversely arrogant male power, and yet she loved being kissed by him, even more, it seemed, with each succeeding kiss.

"Look at me," he ordered quietly.

Leigh, knowing it was useless to resist, allowed her shielding hands to slide away from her face. She gazed up at him, into the stark silver brilliance of his eyes.

"What did Phyllis tell you?"

"Y—you think all you have to do is kiss me, don't you?" Her voice was thready and weak, drained of its strength like her pride and self-respect. She was aware that her soft crepe dress had been shoved up to her thighs in their struggle, but she hadn't the interest to pull it down.

"It does seem to have a softening effect on you," he said, and his voice was a thick, husky whisper of confidence. His eyes swept up and down her body. Then, lithely, he got to his feet, straightening his tie with a steady hand. "Well, are you going to answer me? Or shall I continue breaking down your defenses?"

Leigh's fingers, gaining strength from her humiliation, tugged at the skirt of her dress, pulling it down to her knees. "What is the next step—rape?"

"Come now, Leigh," he rejoined, a smile playing at the corners of his mouth, "we both know that wouldn't be necessary."

She sat up. "Get out," she said tiredly, dispiritedly. "If you want to know what Phyllis told me, ask her."

One of his dark brows raised itself sardonically. "Do you really want to send me back to her tonight?"

"Why should tonight be any different?" she retorted. "And don't flatter yourself that I care one whit where you go when you leave here—just so you leave."

In the stormy silence that followed, his face hardened. Between them there was the knowledge that should he decide to stay, she would not fight him—not for long, at any rate. She was trapped by the force of her own treacherous emotions.

"I'm leaving, Leigh. I'll wish you pleasant dreams." When she did not meet his look, he added, "Good night."

"Good night." Leigh watched the door close behind him, leaving a dead emptiness where his vitality had been. Her earlier feeling of victory following the board meeting was overcome by the strong sense of defeat all around her. So strong that she felt like weeping.

Tomorrow. . . . If only she could find the strength, to-morrow she would leave this place. She would resign, with six weeks left of her probationary period, and go back to Jess Harlan. Back to a safe harbor, back to the confidence and peace of mind she had known before she met Shane Casey.

But she had, finally, faced the fact that it wasn't just the job that held her. It was the man who could arouse in her such a whirlpool of conflicting emotions that she no longer understood herself.

After a while she bestirred herself to get ready for bed. Sleep was long in coming, however. She heard Shane's car leave and—she did not know how much later—return. Her apartment was far enough from the main part of the house that she could hear no other sound after the faint thud of the massive front door closing.

She tossed and turned until exhaustion overtook her in the small hours of the morning. During the next few days she saw little of Shane. Whenever she did, she sensed a rigid reserve in him and was grateful for it. As long as he maintained his distance, there could be no further confrontations between them. But by Friday the strain of his aloofness was beginning to make its presence known in the tautness of her nerves. When Rod asked her to drive into San Antonio for dinner, she accepted with a great deal of relief.

Rod had made reservations at The Stockman, one of the most popular restaurants on the Paseo del Rio. The restaurant was situated on the second level, and their table was in a corner where a large glassed-in section overlooked the river and the narrow walkways that followed its course.

146

They ordered filets mignons and a bottle of Burgundy, both of which were of superb quality.

"You know, I almost didn't ask you out tonight," Rod commented as they lingered over after-dinner coffee. "I didn't think you'd come. You've turned down so many of my invitations. I hope I can interpret your acceptance tonight as a general change in attitude toward me."

"I needed to get away."

"From your job?" Rod's eyebrows shot up. "I can't believe I'm hearing correctly."

Leigh laughed. "I do enjoy a night out occasionally."

"And my company is only incidental?"

His steady blue gaze was making her uncomfortable. "I—I don't know what you want me to say, Rod."

He laid his hand over hers on the tablecloth. "Maybe that you could come to care for me a little."

She extricated her hand and clasped it over her other one in her lap. "Rod, I want you to know I think of you as a friend. But it can never be anything more than that."

He pursed his lips thoughtfully. "I see. Ah, don't tell me. I've lost out to Shane again."

She stiffened. "That is utterly ridiculous."

He cocked his head. "Is it? I know something's going on between the two of you. The tension has been so thick the last week, you could cut it with a knife. I hope you aren't holding out for a commitment from my brother, Leigh, because if you are——"

"I expect nothing from Shane. Nothing. After the first of September I doubt seriously that I'll ever see him again."

Rod looked surprised. "Don't tell me he hasn't spoken to you about renewing your contract."

"He hasn't said a word." She was beginning to believe that Shane had no intention of asking her to stay. She had told herself time and time again that a clean break would be the best thing for everyone. But whenever she thought of leaving the ranch for good, a hard, painful knot formed in the pit of her stomach.

Yet why should she want to stay? Was she a masochist that she enjoyed being alternately dominated and ignored?

How different everything would be if only she could feel that wild-sweet longing for Rod. But when his clear blue eyes rested on her, her heart did not stir, her pulses did not pound. She sought to push these distressing thoughts aside as she realized Rod had spoken again. "What? I'm sorry. My mind was wandering."

Rod looked puzzled for a moment. "I asked if you'd had a chance to talk to Shane about allowing me to my land."

Did she imagine it, or was an intimation of Rod's deep feelings for her always followed by a suggestion that she intervene with Shane in the matter of his land? She lifted her coffee cup in both hands, sipping slowly, and studied him from beneath sooty lashes. For a man who had just been told by a woman for whom he claimed to care deeply that she could never return those feelings, Rod looked remarkably unperturbed. Oh, there was that little frown between his eyebrows, but that had only appeared when he mentioned his land. She was convinced that Rod did not love her, that his unsubtle hints that she meant something to him were nothing more than attempts to butter her up because he thought she had some influence with his brother. It occurred to her that she really did not know Rod very well. He was usually charming and pleasant, but occasionally she had had the feeling that this facade was covering something very different underneath, as Shane had once told her. She had no idea what Rod wanted from life; she had never heard him speak of anything that he would like to do or how he would like to spend his time.

"I—I did speak to him once about what he is doing—refusing to allow you to sell your land. It had no effect on him. He feels it would be a mistake. He intimated that your father would not have approved."

"Our father is dead," Rod said with impatience.

"Maybe you should give it a year or two before you bring it up again. Things may look different then. You may even be glad Shane didn't let you sell when you wanted to."

The look he gave her was, for a fleeting moment, wild

148

with terror, before the dark lashes came down, hooding the blue eyes. "I don't have a year or two." There was such stark finality in the tone that Leigh felt an apprehensive chill.

"What is it, Rod? You sound so desperate."

"What? Oh—" He laughed, but it sounded hollow. "Don't mind me. I'm in one of my self-pitying moods. It will pass. Would you like some more wine, a brandy, anything before we go?"

She shook her head and they left the restaurant. Outside, Rod said, "Let's walk along the river for a little while before we start back."

"All right." But Leigh's further attempts at conversation were met with monosyllables. Soon she said she was tired and would like to start for the ranch, and he agreed.

They had left Rod's car on a dark side street. As they approached the car Leigh noticed a man slouched against a storefront, smoking a cigarette. When they stopped beside the car, the man glanced in their direction and flipped the cigarette into the street. Rod was bending over, trying to fit the key into the lock in the shadowy light. Uneasy, Leigh looked over her shoulder and saw a second man step from a black doorway. Both men were burly-looking and wore dark trousers and tight T-shirts. They walked toward the car.

"Rod—" But she hadn't time to say any more, for suddenly she was pushed roughly aside and the two men grabbed Rod. One of them held his arms behind him while the other hit him in the face.

Leigh screamed and glanced about wildly for help. She saw no one else on the dark street. She heard Rod's loud grunt as his attacker gave him a fierce blow to the stomach. Then Rod slumped against the car as the two men ran down the street and disappeared around the corner.

Leigh ran to his side. "Rod! Rod, can you hear me?"

He was bent over the hood, head down. He raised his head slowly with both hands braced against the fender and gasped, "The keys. I dropped them on the sidewalk."

She searched near the car and saw the keys against the curb. Glancing furtively over her shoulder, panic threatening, she found the right key, fumbled it into the lock on the passenger side, and opened the door. Then she took Rod's arm and helped him to the car, where he sank into the seat with another loud groan.

Leigh's mind was racing. She had just realized that the two attackers hadn't asked for money. They hadn't even taken Rod's wallet from his hip pocket. What had they wanted? It didn't make any sense. Maybe her screams had frightened them away before they had time to take Rod's money.

The dome light revealed a trickle of blood in one corner of Rod's mouth and a cut over his left eyebrow. "We'll find a hospital—" she began.

Rod shook his head slowly, as if he were trying to focus in a fog. "No—nothing's broken. I'll be all right." He laid his head against the seat.

"Are you sure?"

"Yes."

He closed his eyes, and Leigh stood at the open car door, frowning, wondering if she should ignore him and look for a hospital anyway. Then, glancing again with apprehension along the dark street, she shut the passenger door, hurried around to the driver's side, and got in. She pulled away from the curb. "Do you know where the police station is?"

Rod's head came off the seat abruptly. "Why?"

She had stopped for a red light. She turned to look into his battered face. "We have to report this, Rod. I think I might be able to identify one of them if I saw him again."

"No!" His tone was adamant and frightened.

The light turned green and Leigh swung right on the street that had brought them into the city earlier. "The police might be able to find them if we report the attack right away."

"No!" he repeated in the same urgent way. "No police. Drive straight to the ranch, Leigh. Don't stop for anything."

"But—"

"Dammit! If you can't do as I say, pull over and I'll drive."

Rod was getting so agitated that he frightened her. He was certainly in no condition to drive. What if he passed out? "I'll take you to the ranch," she said finally, and he slumped back against the seat again, eyes closed.

On the long drive, Rod seemed to sleep at intervals, but every time she stopped for a light, he was instantly alert and peering about for familiar landmarks, as if he had to keep reassuring himself. When they finally did arrive at the ranch house, she stopped the car in front and took Rod's arm to help him inside. As they stepped into the foyer the study door opened and Shane came toward them. By that time, Rod's left eye was swollen shut and there was an ugly bruise at his temple.

Shane took in his brother's appearance and his brows drew together in a furious scowl. "What in the name of—"

"Are you satisfied now, Shane?" Rod's one good eye glared at his brother furiously. Leigh stared at him. What was he talking about? He must be delirious. Maybe he was more seriously hurt than she had realized.

"Two men attacked him," Leigh said to Shane.

Shane's expression was anxious. "Were you hurt?"

She shook her head. "They didn't even look at me after they pushed me aside to get to Rod. They just kept beating him, Shane, and they never said a word. They didn't even ask for money. I screamed, and that must have frightened them away."

Rod's face suddenly went white and Shane caught him and led him into the study, where he made him lie down on the leather couch. Leigh followed them. "I wanted to take him to a hospital—or to the police station. He wouldn't let me."

Shane looked down at his brother with a troubled expression. "You did the right thing." He glanced at Leigh. "I'm sorry you were put through this. Rod should never have taken you to San Antonio. I'll take care of him now."

It was a clear dismissal, but Leigh hesitated, wanting to ask questions. How could he say she had done the right thing in not going to the police? And why should Rod not have taken her to San Antonio?

Shane walked over to her and put a hand on her shoulder, squeezing lightly. There was no passion in his touch, only a concern for her that was reflected in his gray eyes. "I may have to go to Dallas for a day or two," he said suddenly. "Maggie will know where to reach me if a problem with one of the horses should arise."

She nodded, looking at him uncomprehendingly.

And still his hand rested on her shoulder. "Leigh, you are not to mention to anyone what happened tonight. Do you understand?"

"Yes," she said quietly, although she understood nothing.

His hand dropped away. "Get some rest now, and don't worry about Rod. I'll take care of everything."

TEN

Leigh and José sat atop the corral fence and laughed at the roan mare's colt learning to walk without his casts.

"He tries to dance, señorita!" José whooped as the colt staggered first to one side and then the other, while the mare followed along, nudging him with her nose. "He will end in the circus, yes?"

Leigh grinned. "No, José. That colt will race one day. Look at those legs."

José nodded happily. "You fixed his legs, all right. You smart señorita, Doctor Leigh." The Mexican man's dark eyes rested on her in open admiration. Ever since he'd learned of the school board's decision to promote Manuel to the fourth-grade class, José had lost no opportunity to praise her. He had even credited her with obtaining the tutor who came to the ranch to help with Manuel's reading three afternoons a week. But Leigh had set him straight about that. It had been all of Shane's doing.

Leigh watched the colt fall and get immediately to his feet again. She had studied his front legs from every angle since she and José had removed the casts an hour earlier. There had been a noticeable straightening of the limbs; surgical stapling would not be necessary. Her decision to use the casts had saved the colt from an ignoble future.

"Mr. Shane will be very grateful when he sees him," José predicted. "I am surprised he hasn't been here to check on him already."

"Maggie said he and Rod returned very late last night." The morning after Rod's attack, the two had gone to Dallas "to see Mr. Shane's lawyer on business," Maggie had explained to anyone who asked. Leigh did not know the

153

real reason for the sudden trip, but suspected it had something to do with Rod's beating. She was not even sure that Maggie had been told of the beating, since Rod and Shane had evidently left without seeing her. Shane had pinned a note to the kitchen bulletin board telling Maggie where they'd be staying in Dallas.

Leigh climbed down from the corral fence. "I think I'll have an early lunch, José. We still have to give parasite inoculations to the horses in the south pasture. Do you think we might do it this afternoon?"

José grinned down at her from atop the corral. "I will have the medicine ready for you when you return."

"Good. I'll be back by one." She went to the house, where Rod met her in the foyer.

His swollen eye had gone down, but there were still areas of discoloration around it. Leigh wondered how he had explained that to Maggie. In spite of the black-and-blue marks, however, Rod was in excellent spirits. "I was just going out to search for you."

Leigh looked him over, then said, "I think you're going to live. What did you want to see me about?"

"To tell you my good news. Shane finally agreed to let me sell my share of the ranch."

"What? But he was so opposed to it."

Rod thrust his hands into his trousers' pockets and said expansively, "He changed his mind. That's why we went to Dallas. To have Shane's lawyer draw up the papers."

"But who's the buyer?"

"Shane is. He's buying the land, the cattle, everything. I'm a free man now, Leigh."

Leigh was not surprised to learn that Shane was the buyer. He might have given in to Rod's selling the land, but he would never allow it to pass out of the family.

"You seem very pleased," she said. "What will you do now?"

He shrugged. "Take a vacation first. Maybe in the South Pacific. Then I'm thinking of moving to Houston." He gestured offhandedly. "At least I've got some breathing space now. I have plenty of time to decide how to invest the money."

Breathing space? she thought. What an odd way of putting it. It seemed to Leigh that the beautiful rolling hills and green pastures of the Casey Ranch provided all the breathing space anyone could wish for. But of course Rod had never loved the land as Shane did. Still, it seemed strange to Leigh that he could leave all this without a pang.

"Do you know yet when you'll be leaving?"

"Soon. As soon as I can get a passport. A week or two, probably."

She extended her hand. "I wish you luck, Rod."

Rod eyed the hand with a wry smile before shaking it. "So we have regressed to hand-shaking, have we?" But the tone was good-natured, almost absentminded, as if his thoughts were already in another place, waiting for his body to catch up.

"We never really progressed much beyond that stage," she returned.

"Yeah, I guess you're right. I had bigger ideas once or twice, but you never shared them, did you."

She laughed. "Don't look so downtrodden. You know you don't mean it."

He bent to give her a quick kiss on the cheek. "You're a good kid, Leigh." He left her to go outside, whistling.

When Leigh returned to the barn at one, the office door was open. She went in, expecting to find José, but it was Shane who was seated at the desk, going through one of the folders. He looked up and closed the folder, leaning back in the creaking swivel-chair.

"I was looking for José," she began, stammering a little, feeling stupidly shaken by this first sight of him after three days.

"He hasn't come back from lunch. Sit down. I have something to say to you."

She took a chair opposite the desk.

"I've seen the colt. He looks splendid. You did a fine job on him, and I want to thank you."

Nervously she fingered a button on her cotton shirt. "It was only common veterinary practice." But she felt her cheeks grow warm with pleasure at the praise. Maybe this

155

would make him give serious consideration to renewing her contract. Now would be the perfect time to bring it up. But he didn't. He just sat, gazing at her.

"I talked to Rod before lunch," she said. "You've made him very happy."

He sat forward in the chair, elbows on the desk, the lips, which had softened for a moment, hardening. "Rod may be happy about our bargain; I'm not. But there was nothing else to be done. I finally saw that when those goons attacked him."

"What did that have to do with selling the land?"

He made a sound of disgust. "Everything."

When he was silent for a moment, she said, "I didn't mean to pry."

He ran long fingers through his dark hair. "You're not. In fact, I think you have a right to know what's been going on. Rod has a problem, Leigh. He gambles. Oh, I don't mean just a friendly card game now and then. I mean the big stuff. Before I realized it, he owed almost a hundred and fifty thousand in gambling debts to a San Antonio syndicate. I've bailed him out several times in the past, but not to the tune of that much money."

Leigh stared at him. "Then . . . that's why those men beat him. They were working for the syndicate."

He nodded grimly. "I thought I'd bought him some time. Do you remember the night of our barbecue? They called the house that night. I took the call in my study and made an appointment to talk to them. I drove into San Antonio after midnight to meet with them."

Leigh was remembering that night. Would she ever forget it? The night Shane had kissed her in the dark courtyard, the night he came to her apartment and tried the door that she had locked against him. And then he had left the house, and she had lain in bed, miserable, sure he was going to Phyllis. But he was saying that he had gone to San Antonio to meet with the syndicate men. She remembered Shane's footsteps on the gravel outside her bedroom window, and Rod calling to him: *I'll go with you.* Rod's suggesting that he accompany Shane had seemed odd at the time. Now that she knew where Shane had been going, it made perfect sense—along with other things. Shane's veiled warnings to her about Rod. His anger over the card game the night of the barbecue.

"I told them Rod needed time," he was saying. "I said I was trying to arrange a loan for him. They said they'd take the message to their boss, that we'd be hearing from them." He made a sardonic sound. "The next thing we knew, two of them jumped Rod on that San Antonio street. Their crude idea of a message—but certainly clear enough." He took in Leigh's shocked expression.

"No wonder he didn't want me to go to the police."

"Thank God you listened to him," he said vehemently. "If you'd brought the police into it, they might have killed Rod."

"I—I had no idea."

"I know. You thought I was being stubborn and heartless. Well, maybe I was. But I hoped if I kept refusing to consent to selling the land, Rod would come to his senses. I was wrong. He just kept gambling at every opportunity, trying to make up the losses. That rarely works when a man gets as desperate as Rod was." He sighed. "He says he's learned his lesson now, promised to invest the rest of the money. I'll believe him when I see it."

Leigh could not meet his gaze. She didn't know what to say to him. He *had* been acting in Rod's best interest, and she had accused him of trying to run other people's lives. Everything was so confused. She had misjudged him on this one point, but did that mean she had misjudged him in other areas? She didn't think so. He was still proud, arrogant, imposing his will on others—and not to be trusted entirely. Not by her, anyway.

She was relieved when José appeared. She excused herself and felt Shane's intense gaze on her as she left the office.

After that brief moment in the barn office when he had complimented her on her care of the colt, Shane retreated once more behind a wall of cold indifference—as far as Leigh was concerned. By contrast he seemed unusually short of temper with José and the other hired men. Even Maggie noticed it. Two days later, when Leigh went into the kitchen in search of a glass of iced tea after a long, hot day of working outdoors, the housekeeper said, "Have you and Mr. Shane had a fight?"

Leigh took a paper napkin from the holder on the kitchen table and blotted the perspiration on her forehead. "What gave you that idea?"

Maggie set a tall glass of iced tea in front of her. "The way you're both behaving lately. You acting like you'll go through the ceiling if anybody so much as says boo. And Mr. Shane stalking around with a thundercloud over him, snapping everybody's head off."

"You're imagining things."

"Hah!" Maggie snorted. "I'm not a fanciful person. No, something's going on. Mr. Shane's not himself."

"I don't pretend to understand Shane's moods," Leigh said impatiently.

"That right?" retorted Maggie, her hazel eyes bright with curiosity. "Well, I been putting two and two together."

Leigh took a long swallow of the cold, sweet tea and did not answer.

"I got to thinking," Maggie went on, as if to herself, "that since you came, Phyllis Calhoun hasn't been hanging around the ranch so much."

Leigh smiled. "And you imagine the two things are connected?"

"Could be," said Maggie blandly.

"Did it ever occur to you that Shane and Phyllis might prefer the privacy of her place for their meetings?"

"It did," Maggie admitted, "but I heard a rumor yesterday that Phyllis won't be teaching in San Lorenzo next year."

"Where did you hear that?"

Maggie shrugged. "In the grocery store."

Leigh laughed. "Maggie, even if it's true, it could mean a lot of things." It could mean that Phyllis had decided to change her tactics with Shane and play harder to get. It could also mean that Phyllis was planning another career in the near future—as Shane's wife.

Maggie faced her, hands on hips. "I think it means that

Mr. Shane's eye has fallen elsewhere, and Phyllis has finally realized he's not going to marry her."

Leigh shook her head helplessly. "Do you really think Shane is interested in *me*? You couldn't be more wrong. Shane not only has no personal interest in me, he has no professional interest either. He hasn't renewed my contract, so I'll be leaving the ranch the first of September."

"What!" Maggie was clearly disconcerted by this information. "You mean he hasn't said a word about you staying on?"

"That's what I mean," Leigh said flatly.

"But"—the housekeeper's look was troubled—"I was so sure he was finally getting serious about someone." She shook her head sadly. "He needs to settle down. He needs a wife and children."

"Oh, Maggie." Leigh's smile was indulgent. "You still believe in fairy tales, don't you? Shane Casey is the most self-sufficient man I've ever known. He doesn't need anything or anyone."

"He's just a man," Maggie pronounced, "and he needs a woman's love and care."

Later, in her apartment, Jess Harlan telephoned. Why hadn't she written in more than two weeks? he wanted to know. How was she? How was her job? Still brooding over her conversation with Maggie, Leigh admitted to her guardian that she would probably be moving back to Oklahoma soon. She asked him to be on the lookout for another position for her. Jess Harlan was not sympathetic. She wasn't becoming a quitter, was she? She had to fight harder if she wanted to keep her job. Leigh's reply was noncommittal, and she knew, when she'd hung up, that she had not satisfied the professor.

There was no way Leigh could explain things to Uncle Jess. Too much had happened that summer. The relationship that had developed with Shane Casey was too fraught with pitfalls to continue indefinitely. He wanted—if he wanted anything at all from her—merely to possess her body for momentary pleasure. She wanted much more. Two such opposing desires could not be reconciled. This was becoming more clear to her with each passing day.

It was a long, restless evening for Leigh. The small apartment that had, at first, seemed so perfectly suited to her needs felt like a confining prison. She showered and retired early, hoping to drown her melancholy mood in sleep. But sleep would not come. At last she arose from her tumbled bed, slipped on scuffs and a light robe, and left the apartment quietly to walk for a while in the shadowy courtyard.

As she walked, her thoughts continued in the same repetitive cycle they had followed all evening. She had only three weeks left at the ranch. She tried to tell herself that her feeling of desolation was absurd. She would still have a home with Jess Harlan for as long as she needed it, and she had a profession that paid well and work that she enjoyed. Less than three months ago that had seemed enough.

But she had changed. She was not the same naive, trusting, self-confident person she had been at the beginning of the summer. Now she was a woman filled with uncertainty and a desperate unhappiness. For this she could thank Shane Casey.

She paused in her pacing as she caught the faint odor of tobacco. Then she saw the glowing end of a cheroot as it was dropped to the ground where it was extinguished under a boot heel. Shane stepped from the deep shadows into the faint, eerie light of the full moon.

"I didn't mean to intrude," she said hesitantly. "I thought I was alone."

"Everyone is alone," he said with a sarcastic edge to the words.

"Is that what you think?"

"I always have." He seemed to hesitate, then shrugged and took her arm lightly. "I will join you in your walk."

Leigh drew back. "I—I was about to go inside when I saw you."

"Not now." The tone was impervious. "I have something to say to you."

It did not seem worth an argument, so she began to walk along beside him, being careful to leave enough space between them so that their arms did not touch.

"Phyllis will not be teaching the fourth grade in San Lorenzo next term. Because of your interest in Manuel, I thought you would be relieved to know that."

"Yes," she admitted, "I am. Will Phyllis be teaching another grade?"

"I don't know. She is going back to Dallas."

"I see." What did he expect her to say?

"After I discovered the gossip she was spreading, I thought it best for all concerned that she leave San Lorenzo. It took some doing, but she eventually came to see my point of view."

Leigh tensed. She did not want to discuss what Phyllis had told her—with Shane or anyone else. Nothing but pain could come from raking up the past. "I believe I'll go in now."

He stopped beside her and his hand gripped her arm. "Not until I'm finished. And don't bother crying or pleading—or anything else. You are going to hear what I have to say."

Crying or pleading! She had no intention of doing either, "Go ahead," she retorted stiffly.

"At the age of seventeen Manuel's mother was a beautiful, fun-loving girl. In those days, the Mexicans who lived on the ranch still had frequent feasts and celebrations. There was always much drinking and dancing, and María was the best, the most exciting dancer of them all. Young men came from all over the neighborhood to watch her dance, all hoping for a chance or a few minutes alone with her. She was an outrageous flirt and reveled in all the attention she got."

"So, of course, everything that happened was her own fault!" Leigh burst out, infuriated by the insinuation behind his words.

His hand on her arm tightened. "Let me finish. As I was saying, María was a flirt, but she had a proud, cagey father, who was determined that she would go to her marriage a virgin. He rarely let her out of his sight. Moments alone with María were difficult to come by. I was in a position to know, for I tried very hard to arrange such a meeting."

"Naturally," said Leigh between clenched teeth.

"*Naturally*, yes," Shane returned. "That is precisely the right word. What I felt for María was the natural physical attraction of a healthy young man for a beautiful girl. The attraction was heightened, I am sure, by the fact that her father's close surveillance put María tantalizingly out of reach. Or so I thought."

"Phyllis was right," fumed Leigh. "You found a way to—"

He uttered an impatient curse and, still gripping her arm, propelled her across the courtyard to a lounge near the pool. He pushed her down on the lounge and stood over her. "Now, sit there and be quiet until I'm finished."

Shivering, Leigh straightened her disarranged robe, pulling it over her legs, and remained rigidly still.

"One day José Gomez came to the house and asked to see me. I didn't know José well then because he was employed on another ranch, but I knew he was one of the young men who had been courting María. We went into my study, and José told me that María had been slipping out at night, after her father was asleep, to meet him, and that she was pregnant with his child. He was only nineteen himself and was understandably frightened at the prospect of breaking the news to María's formidable father. He wanted me to serve as mediator—explain the situation to the old man and arrange for him and María to marry as soon as possible. María's father was fit to be tied, but he had little choice except to agree to the marriage. José came to work for me, and Manuel was born seven months later."

An almost unearthly silence followed, broken only when Leigh drew in a deep breath. "Phyllis said—"

"Phyllis is an insanely possessive woman," Shane retorted brutally. "Rumors that I could be Manuel's father have circulated around San Lorenzo at regular intervals ever since he was born. It was well-known that I frequently attended the Mexican dances and"—there was an uncaring shrug—"certain of my . . . past relationships have probably added fuel to the fire. It was inevitable that

162

Phyllis would hear the rumors and believe them. None of which concerns me very much."

Leigh ran her tongue over dry lips. "Why are you telling me all this?"

"Because I want you to know that you can be wrong about something. You have an unattractive habit of setting yourself up as judge and jury over other people's lives, Leigh. And you have a remarkable facility for lying."

"That isn't true!" Suddenly Leigh was on her feet, unable to bear any more in stricken immobility. "When have I ever lied to you?"

He was so close to her that she could smell the faint aroma of tobacco clinging to his clothes. "Not to me, Leigh," he said with quiet intensity, "to yourself. What were you telling yourself as you paced, like a caged cat, about the courtyard earlier? That you want to leave here? That you despise me and can't wait to get away from me? Weren't you bemoaning the fact that your stupid, sentimental, romantic dream had been shattered—the dream that some day a white knight was going to sweep you off your feet and carry you away to never-never land? Plain, ordinary human frailty and passion were never any part of that dream, were they, Leigh?"

Hot tears rushed to Leigh's eyes as his remorseless words hammered at her. "You're cruel. I—I hate you—"

With a low growl, he jerked her against him. "You are still lying to yourself."

Her heart lurched and with a cry that seemed to come from deep inside her, she fought him with a strength she did not know she possessed. He shoved her back down on the lounge, forcing her into a supine position, and stretched his hard length beside her, pinning her down with his leg, effectively immobilizing her by holding her wrists against the lounge cushion on either side of her head.

"You disgust me!" she spat at him.

His mouth assaulted hers with cruel force. She clamped her teeth shut against him, but the assault continued until her futile struggling ceased and then it became quieter, gentler. As his moist, warm mouth explored hers, Leigh

163

felt a seeping languor begin to sap her of the desire to resist.

His mouth left her bruised lips and searched for the hollow at the base of her throat, his tongue flicking lightly. His fingers entwined themselves in her hair, then dropped lower where her robe had been flung wide and nothing separated her clamoring flesh from his touch except the single gossamer layer of her nightgown. But this was pushed aside, too, and his hand came in contact with her breast, and she uttered a moan of mingled need and self-loathing. Then his mouth found the soft fullness of her breast and set her afire. She heard his heart racing, his breathing thicken. Her hands shook as she buried them in his thick, dark hair, pressing him closer to her. She surrendered hungrily to his lovemaking, her hands slipping inside his shirt and tracing the hard outlines of his muscled back.

Shane made a triumphant sound and lifted his head to let his gaze play over the pale curves of her body in the moonlight. "Your words may lie, but your body does not." He bent his head to kiss her neck, his lips brushing her bare shoulders hotly. "Oh, Leigh . . . Leigh. . . ."

A flame shot through her and she groaned, her hands running through his tousled hair. For a moment she let herself drown in the delirium of her emotions, wanting him with such wild unreason that she barely heard his muttered endearments over the roaring in her ears.

"You've been driving me crazy all summer," he said thickly. "When I saw you walking in the courtyard tonight, I knew I had to have you."

Alarm bells rang in her head, and she closed her eyes, shutting out the staggering desire in his face. He had seen her come into the courtyard; he had followed her, intending—by whatever means—to break down her resistance and make love to her.

He had become still suddenly, and she felt his smoldering look on her face. She opened her eyes, stiffening beneath him.

"Say it, Leigh. Say you want me as much as I want you."

She felt tears trickling down her cheeks. "And then,"

she said bitterly, "if I please you well enough, you may decide to renew my contract."

His hands gripped her shoulders with sudden violence. She looked up into a face torn by rage and passion.

"Is that the price of your capitulation?"

"Get your hands off me!" she spat at him, fury filling her, beating hotly at her temples. "Why do you have to twist everything—make everything cheap?"

He was very still, staring at her for a long moment. The hard features froze into a mask; the gray eyes narrowed. Then, abruptly, he let her go, drawing himself away from her, standing beside the lounge, his body trembling with suppressed need and rising fury. "Get up before I strangle you."

Shaking, she sat up, tugging at her gown, pulling the robe close about her. She got to her feet unsteadily.

"What are you waiting for?" he demanded.

She straightened, exerting every ounce of strength she had to meet his contemptuous look. "For you to fire me. Isn't that what's coming next?"

"Don't look to me for an easy way out, Leigh," he snarled. "I intend to stand by my bargain until the bitter end if it kills me—if it kills both of us."

She drew a long, shuddering breath, oddly relieved and let down at the same time.

"Get your things together. We're going to Cozumel on Friday."

She stared at the hard mask of his face. "Cozumel," she said blankly. "But isn't that in Mexico?"

"It's an island in the Caribbean off the coast of Mexico."

"But—you said 'we.' Do you mean you and I are going to Cozumel?"

He made a bitterly contemptuous sound. "You and I, yes. That is the meaning of 'we,' I believe."

"Why are you doing this?" she asked tiredly.

"Doing what, Leigh? I have a chance to buy an excellent horse. He happens to be on Cozumel. Is it so strange that I would want to look at him before making an offer? I expect my veterinarian to go with me."

"Do I have a choice?"

"Certainly. You can quit and run back to Jess Harlan like a peevish child whose will has been thwarted."

Slink away like a whipped dog, she thought. That's what he expected her to do. He thought she couldn't take any more. "I'll be ready to leave for Cozumel Friday," she said. Head held high, she walked away from him across the courtyard, the fresh tears that were streaming down her face mercifully hidden from his gaze.

ELEVEN

The flight from Texas to Mérida, where they had a short stopover, was strained. Neither Shane nor Leigh made much of an effort at conversation; in fact, they had had little to say to each other since that night by the pool. Now Leigh was convinced that Shane did not intend to renew her contract. If he had wanted to discuss it, there had been ample opportunity. With only fifteen days left before the first of September, she hoped their uneasy truce would continue until she could leave the ranch for good.

As the plane taxied to a halt on the runway, Shane turned to her. "We'll be here for twenty minutes. There will be time to stretch your legs if you'd like."

"I think I'll stay here."

He shrugged and, unbuckling his seat belt, stood. "I'll phone the Cozumel airport to let Salvanto know our flight has been slightly delayed."

As he strode away from her down the aisle, Leigh rested her head against the seat and closed her eyes, which felt hot and gritty. In the past few days she had become accustomed to this feeling—nerves strained so tautly that tears were never very far away. This fragile emotional state was unlike her, and she hated it. Hated herself, too, for what she had become. What had happened to the self-assurance and independence she had cultivated so carefully? How had she been reduced to this weak, foolish female whom she despised? Only a weak fool would fall in love with such an arrogant, domineering man like Shane Casey. Only a fool would feel anything but revulsion for a man who treated women as objects to be possessed.

There had been a time when she would have given anything to know what she now knew—that Shane was not Manuel's father, that whatever there had once been between Shane and Phyllis, it was over. But the knowledge had come too late. Too much had happened between her and Shane for it to make any difference. She had been hurt, perhaps beyond healing. And Shane? Beneath that hard, cold exterior had he, too, been hurt? Possibly his ego had been bruised, but if he felt anything beyond that, it was impossible to know.

She sighed raggedly. Only two more weeks of exercising this rigid self-control, of presenting a cool, untroubled face to the world while inside she was a tangle of confused feelings. Surely she could last that long. If she had to fall apart, let it be after she had put several hundred miles between herself and Shane.

Very soon Shane was back, buckling himself into his seat beside her. "I got hold of him. He didn't seem bothered by the delay. Mexicans often aren't as concerned with time as we Americans are. Probably the climate has something to do with that; it's not conducive to hurrying. The heat in this part of the world can be almost unbearable at times. This is the end of the rainy season, though, so hopefully the weather won't be so bad."

"Have you known Ben Salvanto long?"

"Only a couple of years. His interest in quarter horses is more of a hobby than anything else. He owns one of the big hotels on the mainland side of the island. I met him two years ago at a horse auction in Oklahoma City. He bought a colt I had bid on. So now that he's decided to sell the horse, he offered me the first opportunity to buy."

The plane was taxiing for takeoff now and Shane, wearing a tan, western-styled, leisure suit, relaxed in the seat beside her. As long as they were discussing horses they seemed to be able to converse without strain. Leigh found this much preferable to the long silences that had characterized most of the trip.

"Tell me about the horse."

"He has championship bloodlines on both sides. If I find he's lived up to his early promise, I'll buy him. But I want to be sure he's not carrying anything that could infect my

168

herd. Mexican authorities are lax about that sort of thing. I want a clean bill of health before moving him."

Leigh glanced at the carry-on satchel at her feet, which contained a small microscope, chemicals, and other things needed for taking the tests he wanted. "I can run the tests in one day."

"Good. Then we shouldn't have to remain long. Unless you'd like to stay for a few days. Cozumel is a diver's paradise."

"I've never learned to dive. Have you?"

The gray-blue eyes flicked over her briefly. "No, and I understand you have to show evidence of having completed a diving course before they will allow you to rent equipment. They are stricter about rules where people are concerned." He leaned across her to gaze out the window. "Take a look. We're over the Caribbean now."

The water below them was such an unbelievably deep shade of blue that Leigh caught her breath. "It's gorgeous!"

"The Caribbean's the prettiest body of water in the world—except perhaps for the Aegean. They say that once the Caribbean has you in its spell, it never lets you go."

The plane was circling in preparation for descent. "Look at the dazzling whiteness of the beach," Leigh exclaimed. "No wonder people fall in love with this part of the world."

"The Caribbean and white sand," Shane returned. "That's all Cozumel has, but they promote them for all they're worth. In the last few years, a number of hotels have been built on this side and the only town, San Miguel, consists mostly of restaurants and shops that cater to the tourist trade. The interior of the island is a desolate wasteland." A mocking smile flitted across his hard face. "Even paradise is not perfect."

"Maybe you have to have the imperfections," Leigh mused, "before you can truly appreciate the beautiful things."

She felt Shane's gaze upon her. "Maybe you do."

When they deplaned, steaming humidity enveloped them and Leigh's tailored jersey dress clung heavily to her skin.

They were greeted by a slender, dark man who looked to be in his early sixties. His thick black hair was liberally streaked with silver, and his ready smile was genuine.

Shane clapped a hand on the shorter man's shoulder. "Ben! It's good to see you again."

"Welcome, Shane!" Salvanto returned in English that bore hardly the trace of an accent. He turned his smile on Leigh. "Welcome to your lovely lady too."

Shane hastened to correct what seemed to be Salvanto's mistaken impression of the situation. "This is my veterinarian, Ben. Doctor Leigh Alexander."

Salvanto's effusive welcome was not dampened, however. "Welcome to Cozumel, Doctor."

"Leigh, please."

"Good, good. And I am Ben. Now we are all friends, yes?"

Leigh returned the happy smile; indeed, it was impossible not to do so.

"My wife sends her apologies for not being here to greet you also," Salvanto continued as they walked toward the terminal. "She was called away to Mexico City yesterday. Her mother has fallen ill."

"I'm sorry," Shane said. "I hope we didn't keep you from accompanying her."

"No, no." Salvanto shook his head. "She is old. It is her heart, you see. She has these spells often now. My wife will call me if this one seems more critical than the others."

They claimed their luggage and accompanied Salvanto to his station wagon. Shane took a backseat, leaving the place next to their host for Leigh. Soon they were skimming along the narrow highway that hugged the coastline.

"San Miguel," Salvanto said as they approached the island's only settlement. Here the road was bordered by a broad sidewalk and a white seawall on the ocean side and small adobe buildings fronted by a line of palm trees with whitewashed trunks on the town side. The harbor beyond the seawall was dotted with boats of all sizes and descriptions.

The heart of San Miguel was marked by a small plaza

with a raised, circular bandstand. "During the height of the tourist season," Salvanto told them, "native musicians play here every evening."

Their host's hacienda was a half mile beyond San Miguel, a large cream-colored Spanish-style mansion surrounded by several acres of carefully cultivated lawn and with a solid masonry wall enclosing the estate on the three land-sides.

"We have a private beach in back," Salvanto said as he swung the station wagon into the palm-bordered drive. "I hope you will find the time to enjoy it while you are here."

Leigh was given a second-story bedroom with a balcony overlooking the beach. After the maid had left her alone, she admired the dark, carved furniture, the high-beamed ceiling, and the soft yellow bedspread and draperies. She kicked off her high-heeled shoes and slid open the glass door that opened onto the balcony. Stepping out, she moved to the railing and looked down at the blue waves lapping at the white beach below. The house, the view from her balcony—it was like a scene from a romantic movie, almost too beautiful to be real. Yet she had only to look to one side, beyond the estate wall, and see the dead, scrubby landscape, which seemed to go on indefinitely. Cozumel was an island of stark contrasts.

Within minutes the high humidity, along with the intense heat of the sun, had become oppressive. Leigh slipped gratefully back into the air-conditioned bedroom, where she unpacked the few clothes she had brought with her and hung them in the closet. It was not yet six, and Ben had said they would have dinner at eight. Leigh slipped out of the clinging damp crepe dress and stretched across the bed in panties and bra. The somnolent silence, broken only by the faint faraway hum of the air conditioning, had a lulling effect. She drifted into sleep, awaking just in time to bathe and dress for dinner.

She wore a soft blue polyester sundress with narrow straps and backless sandals without hose. She pulled her hair on top of her head, securing it in a loose chignon with combs. Downstairs, one of the maids directed her to

171

the patio in back of the house, where a small table overlooking the beach had been set for three. Shane and their host were already there, having a drink together.

"Would you like something before dinner, Leigh?" Ben asked.

"No, thank you." She walked to the patio wall and looked out where dusk had softened the brilliant colors of sand, sky, and ocean. "You must feel very fortunate, Ben, to live here with all this to look at and enjoy whenever you wish."

Salvanto made a regretful sound. "It is there to enjoy, yes, but the hotel keeps me very busy and sometimes, I confess, I do not even look at it for days at a time. Also, we keep a house in Mexico City, where we often go during the off-season. My wife enjoys the bustle of the city. It gives her a vacation from so much serenity."

Leigh turned around, leaning against the low wall. "I suppose even this can get monotonous after a while. Shane told me there is little on Cozumel except for the tourist industry."

"And one very fine stallion," Shane amended.

Salvanto laughed. "Shane and I visited the stables while you were in your bedroom, Leigh. You will see him tomorrow." He walked to the portable bar that had been set up in a corner of the patio and freshened his drink. Turning, he continued, "But Shane's assessment of our island is an accurate one. A few families scratch out a meager living by farming small acreages, but the land is not fertile and there is not enough rainfall." The shoulders in the white jacket lifted in a gesture of stoic acceptance. "In there"—he gestured in the direction where Leigh had glimpsed the barren landscape from the balcony—"is nothing, except for some ancient Mayan ruins. They are not well-restored, but perhaps in time the archaeologists will turn their attention to our island. At present the ruins are difficult to reach, although if one were determined, they are accessible by Land-Rover or on foot. In fact, there is a small site less than a mile from here."

"Can it be seen from upstairs?" Leigh asked with interest.

"No," Ben said, "but you wouldn't see much, at any rate. Only the remains of a few crumbling buildings and earth mounds. Ah, here is our dinner now."

Ben held Leigh's chair for her, after which the two men were seated and the plump maid named Dorothea began to serve. The main course was chicken, seasoned with a delicious combination of spices and wrapped for baking in banana leaves. There was wine with the meal and, a light pudding for dessert, laced with slivers of pineapple and coconut.

They lingered, sipping the last of the wine and talking about horses. Ben said he was selling all of his except for a few gentle mounts he would keep for his grandchildren to ride when they visited from the mainland. He could not give the horses enough time and attention, so he had decided to get out of the quarter-horse business entirely.

Leigh listened to the men's conversation with half her attention while gazing at the moon-silvered Caribbean below. After a while she excused herself to walk along the beach.

Steps led down from the lawn beyond the patio to the white sand. Leigh removed her sandals and, carrying them, walked barefoot along the water's edge. She prolonged her desultory walk, reluctant to leave the edenic setting, even for the attractive air-conditioned bedroom. At length she heard someone approaching and turned to see Ben Salvanto coming toward her.

"Señorita Leigh," he greeted her, "I thought you might wish some company. I often walk here at night."

He joined her and they strolled slowly. "The sand is still warm to my feet," she murmured after a while. "I know it must be getting late, but this is all new to me. I can't get over the beauty of this place. It's perfect."

Ben chuckled. "The perfect place for lovers, yes, Leigh?"

She laughed. "I'm sure it must be. Shane says divers like it too."

"That is true. We have one of the finest coral reefs in the world. It is famed among scuba enthusiasts. You are a diver, yes?"

She peered at him in the dimness. "No. Why did you think that?"

"Because you seemed so eager to speak of it, but perhaps it was only that you did not wish to continue to talk of lovers." She kicked at the sand, not looking at him now. "I sense that you and Shane have had a quarrel."

She stopped short, staring at the vague outlines of his face in the moonlight. "Are you suggesting—yes, you do think that we are lovers, don't you?"

He cleared his throat—a hesitant, embarrassed sound. "I am sorry, Leigh, but it was a natural assumption, you must agree. You are a beautiful young woman and I have seen a certain look in his eyes when they rest on you."

Leigh started walking again. "I don't know what you think you have seen, Ben, but you are wrong about our relationship. I work for Shane, that's all, and even that is not likely to continue much longer."

He was silent for a long while, walking beside her, and the sound of the surf beat a melancholy rhythm in the background. "Will you indulge an old man for a few minutes longer?"

Leigh took his arm companionably. "You are not an old man, Ben."

"Ah, well. I will be sixty-two my next birthday. My sons are grown and have children of their own. I have lived much longer than you, my dear. Do you know what I have learned in my sixty-two years?"

"What?" she said, smiling.

"That most of the problems between people result from pride. It is a very sterile, fruitless emotion. It should never be allowed to get in the way of love."

Leigh sighed softly. "You are a romantic, Ben." She had a brief impulse to tell him that whatever love there was between her and Shane was all on her side. But the pride he spoke of checked the words. Finally she said, "Tell me, have you and Shane come to an agreement about the horse?"

"We are negotiating, my dear." There was amusement in the tone. "These things take time, and we would not have it any other way. When we do agree on a price, you see, each of us must feel that he has gotten the best of the bargain."

"I see. How long do you think it will take?"

"A few days. Neither of us wants to appear eager to close the deal, for that might give the other an unfair advantage."

"You may be a romantic," she returned, "but I think there is a bit of the cynic in you too."

He laughed. "Most probably. Shall we return to the house now?"

"Yes. I'm tired. I feel as if I could sleep for a week."

"It is the climate. You would grow used to it if you stayed long enough."

They did not see Shane when they returned to the house and Ben said good night to her with a fond look at the bottom of the stairs. For a brief moment, he reminded her of Jess Harlan, and she had a ridiculous desire to hug him. But she merely said, "Good night," and, still carrying her sandals, hurried barefoot up the graciously curving staircase.

She was awakened the next morning by a soft rap at her door, and then Dorothea came in, carrying a breakfast tray. Leigh sat up, yawning, and smoothed sleep-tangled hair away from her face.

"Good morning, Dorothea. Do you spoil all your guests this way? My goodness, you've brought enough for a field hand. Well, I'll do my best."

The plump Mexican woman was setting the tray, which had short legs, on Leigh's lap. As Leigh talked, she kept smiling and bobbing her head. "*Sí, señorita, sí.*" Apparently, she spoke no English at all.

"*Muchas gracias,*" Leigh said and Dorothea left, still bobbing her head and smiling. Leigh ate a piece of toast and a small bowl of fruit compote. Then she lingered over coffee, enjoying the uncommon luxury of having breakfast in bed. But after a while she glanced at her wristwatch and saw it was almost nine. Today she was supposed to run tests on the stallion. Shane, who was an early riser, had probably been up for hours and no doubt was impatiently awaiting her appearance.

She set the breakfast tray aside and threw back the covers. She dressed hurriedly in jeans and a knit shirt. She scrubbed her face and teeth, applied only a dash of lip gloss, and gave her hair a quick brushing before pulling it back and tying it away from her face with a ribbon. Then, picking up the satchel containing the vet supplies, she went downstairs.

Shane and Ben Salvanto were having coffee on the patio.

"I hope I haven't kept you waiting. I don't know when I've slept so soundly."

"Do not concern yourself," Ben said. "There is plenty of time."

In their host's easy smile Leigh recognized the unhurried Mexican approach to life that Shane had described. Shane, however, was clearly impatient to get on with the business that had brought them to Cozumel.

"I'd like to get started on the tests, Ben."

Ben agreed amiably and they left the patio and walked along the narrow path leading to the stable, which was hidden from the house by a long line of trees.

The stallion was magnificent, his gleaming black coat broken only by two white stockings and a narrow blaze of white on his forehead.

"It appears my stableboy has not arrived yet," Ben commented. "He lives in San Miguel. But, this gentleman is going to be a good fellow, aren't you, sir?" He began to stroke the stallion's neck as he talked.

Leigh walked to the stallion's other side and rubbed her hand over his sleek coat. "I don't think he's going to cause any trouble."

Shane cast her a speaking glance. "I'll stay and help her, Ben. I know you want to get to the hotel."

"The hotel will be there whenever I arrive. It doesn't matter."

"Of course, it matters," Leigh protested. "Now, you go do your work, and I'll do mine." She carefully avoided looking at Shane, who was frowning impatiently.

Ben shrugged good-naturedly. "Very well. I will see the two of you at dinner. *Adiós*." He left them.

Leigh stroked the velvet softness of the stallion's nose. "Oh, isn't he a beauty? Do you think Ben would mind if I rode him after we've finished the tests?"

Shane said curtly, "I won't allow you to ride this horse, no matter what he says."

Leigh stiffened at the commanding tone. How he loved to order other people around! She set her satchel down in one corner of the stall and opened it. "Since you don't own this horse yet," she returned, unable to quell her irritation at his imperiousness, "I don't think you have anything to say about it."

He strode toward her, his face set and hard. "Listen to me, you stubborn little idiot. This horse has been broken to ride, but he has been ridden only a few times by the stableboy. He has yet to be trained properly, which is why I am sending him directly from here to my trainer."

She straightened, holding the syringe in her hands, and met his glowering gaze. "He seems gentle enough to me."

She saw the muscles along his arms go rigid and knew that he wanted to shake her, but the arms remained stiffly at his sides. She walked toward the horse.

From behind her he said, "I am ordering you to stay off this horse, Leigh. If you'll take a good look at his eyes, you'll see there's plenty of wildness left in him. Now, let's do the tests and get out of here."

"I am quite capable of doing this on my own."

"Spare me the feminist lecture!" He moved to take hold of the stallion's halter. "Let's get on with it."

She knew it was useless to argue with him, even though the stallion showed no signs of rebellion. She set to work quickly, managing for the most part to ignore Shane, who kept the halter firmly in his grip.

In a short time they were both wet with perspiration, their shirts clinging to their bodies. The air inside the stable was stiflingly hot and heavy with humidity. The tests took the better part of the morning. Fortunately the stallion behaved himself, which expedited the procedures. Nothing questionable showed up in any of the tests.

"He's clean," Leigh said as she gathered up her supplies.

Shane's only response was a disgruntled sound. They walked back to the house together in silence.

After lunch Leigh put on her bikini and a terry cover-up and went to the beach, where she spent the afternoon alternately sunning herself and cooling off in the water. Late in the afternoon, she was stretched out, half-asleep, on a towel spread on the sand when she heard the soft squishing of footsteps approaching. She looked up as Shane, wearing white swimming trunks, spread a towel beside hers.

"I've been watching you from the house. You seemed to be enjoying this so much, I thought I'd try it."

"Has Ben come home yet?"

He sprawled, full-length, on his towel, half-sitting as he braced himself on his elbows. "No. Dorothea says he usually arrives about six."

She was lying on her stomach, her cheek resting on crossed arms, her eyes half closed against the sunlight. "I'll leave the two of you to talk privately before dinner. Perhaps you can come to an agreement about the horse."

"Are you so eager to leave?"

She turned her head so that she could look up at him. He was gazing out over the blue ocean and, for a fleeting moment, her eyes lingered hungrily on the rugged profile, the lean jaw. In that moment she took in the dark hair that curled at the nape of his tanned neck, the strong muscles of his wide shoulders and flat stomach, and the stark contrast of the white trunks. She pulled her eyes away.

"I've done what I came to do. When you and Ben agree on a price, there is no reason for us to stay any longer, is there?"

The sun was an orange ball near the horizon, spilling liquid gold on the sea. His eyes were narrowed against the sunlight, the dark lashes lowered over the hard cheekbones. "I suppose not."

There was a speculative slowness in the words that Leigh didn't understand. Maybe he would be content to idle away another week or two here, but she did not think

178

she could bear the physical closeness that was almost impossible to avoid, since the two of them were alone in the house, except for the servants, much of the time.

He turned to catch her glance. "Are you becoming bored already? Would you like me to take you into San Miguel tomorrow? I'm sure Ben would be happy to loan us a vehicle."

Leigh shrank from the idea of several hours spent in his company without even the privacy of her bedroom for relief from the electric tension his presence brought with it. "No, thank you. I'd prefer to stay here."

His narrowed eyes studied her face for a moment. "Have you—made any plans for the future?" Did he actually think she would plead with him to be allowed to keep her job at the ranch? Did he think he had reduced her to that?

"Nothing definite," she replied coldly. She slipped her arms into the cover-up and buttoned it in front.

"Leigh, I'd like you to understand something. I haven't mentioned renewing your contract because"—he seemed to be searching for the right words—"the way things stand, I'm not sure it would be a good idea. For a while, I hoped—" He was suddenly unwilling to meet her look.

But she knew what he was trying to say. His actions during the summer had made it all too plain. He had hoped to keep her on the ranch, not just as an employee, but as his mistress. In the beginning he had probably thought she would jump at the chance to offer her body in exchange for a secure position as ranch veterinarian.

"You've made it quite clear what you hoped for," she retorted, getting to her feet and shaking the sand from her towel with unsteady hands. "I hope I've made it equally clear that I'm not interested."

Shane drew his brows together and Leigh saw the tightening of his wide, tanned shoulders. "There have been times, Leigh, when your behavior showed quite a bit more than mere interest. If you weren't so hung up—"

"Oh, that's right!" she cut in bitterly. "Any girl who doesn't tumble into bed with Shane Casey at the first opportunity is undoubtedly a bundle of hang-ups!" Yet even as she said the angry words, she knew Shane's remark was true enough. She wanted him. More than that, she wanted his love . . . his children . . . but she knew from his rigid self-control that all she had right now was his furious anger. Perhaps, she thought cynically, even that is better than the cold indifference he has shown in the past few days.

The way he was looking at her now was certainly not indifferent. The gray eyes glinted with dark emotions that were almost tangible in the air between them. It made her feel breathless. "I've had enough sun for today. I'll see you at dinner." She hurried toward the house, trembling at the explosive fury they seemed to arouse in each other whenever they were alone together. She suddenly felt like a prisoner on the island. There was nowhere for her to go to get away from Shane.

She took several deep breaths as she crossed the patio, forcing her rioting thoughts to slow down. It couldn't take more than another day or two for Shane and Ben to come to an agreement about the horse. In the meantime she would simply avoid him as much as possible.

TWELVE

Leigh's resolution proved harder to keep than she had imagined. In order to avoid running into Shane, she spent much of the next day in her bedroom, reading. She probably would not have stayed outside long, in any case; the heat continued unbroken. She did not know how Shane spent his time. That day passed, too, without Ben and Shane reaching an agreement.

The next morning Leigh arose early and, tired of looking at the four pale yellow walls of her bedroom—lovely as the room was—she went downstairs for breakfast. When she entered the dining room, Dorothea greeted her with smiles and a tumble of Spanish, none of which Leigh understood. Finally she managed to glean the information that both Ben and Shane had left the hacienda earlier. Perhaps, she thought hopefully, they were closing their business deal—signing a contract, transferring the stallion's registration papers.

After breakfast she decided to walk about the estate before the day became too hot for walking. She was wearing shorts and a halter, for she had discovered the less one wore on Cozumel the more comfortable one would be. This morning, however, the sun was hidden behind a dark haze of blackly outlined clouds, and it was cooler than it had been since their arrival.

She ended her walk at the stable and went in to say hello to the stallion. He seemed happy to have human companionship, and she stayed for some time in his stall, stroking and talking to him. He was by far the most beautiful specimen she had ever seen, the sort of animal every horse-lover dreams of owning.

"How I would love to ride you," she crooned. Then she realized that this idea had been in the back of her mind ever since she discovered that Ben and Shane were away. Nor had the stableboy arrived yet, and if he kept to his schedule of the last two days, he wouldn't appear much before noon. She had seen a saddle and saddle blanket hanging on the wall outside the stall. The circumstances were too propitious for her to deny any longer the desire to ride the stallion.

Without stopping to think it through, she saddled the horse and led him from the stable. Looking around her, she saw a gate in the south section of the estate wall and, still leading the stallion, she went to the gate and opened it. A narrow path led away from the wall through the scrubby brush toward the interior of the island. The path looked smooth enough for easy riding.

Mounting, she pulled gently on the reins and the stallion started, in an easy trot, down the path. He responded beautifully to each tug of the reins and Leigh began to feel quite smug. How wrong Shane had been to say the horse's lack of training had left him with a wild streak. Apparently this was an extremely intelligent horse.

Gentle raindrops were beginning to fall and Leigh raised her face to the sky, reveling in the rain, which was cooling the scorched landscape. She rode on as the rain came down faster, heedless of her wet hair and clothing. She would turn back soon, she told herself. A little rain never hurt anyone, and the stallion didn't seem to mind it either.

She was talking to the horse—silly, meaningless phrases in a soft voice meant to soothe away whatever uneasiness he might be feeling—when she saw the crumbling pillars of an ancient stone-structure to her right and, beyond that, a mound of dirt and brush with what looked like part of a roof rising out of it. She had happened upon the Mayan ruins Ben had spoken of. In her excitement at the discovery she dug her bare knees into the stallion's flanks to urge him forward. At the same moment a large lizard spurted across the path in front of them.

Without warning, the stallion reared wildly, and Leigh,

who was totally unprepared for the reaction, tumbled from his back and landed in a scratchy clump of twigs and leaves. A sharp pain shot through her ankle.

She grabbed the ankle with both hands and, blinking back tears, groaned loudly. Then she heard a sudden pounding of hooves and, looking up, saw the stallion racing back along the path the way they had come.

"Come back here!"

But even as she yelled after him, he was disappearing over a gently sloping hill. The rain was pelting down in earnest now, and a low, deep roll of thunder filled the sky. When Leigh tried to get to her feet, she discovered her ankle was already swelling and the pain, when she put her weight on it, was sharp. It was almost a mile back to the hacienda and the rain was coming down in such torrents that it was difficult to see the path any longer.

Leigh stood with her weight on one leg, water running off her hair and dripping in her face, her clothes plastered to her body, and glanced about frantically for shelter. The only possibility was the crumbling Mayan structure to the right of the path. Gritting her teeth, she limped toward it. A small portion of the roof remained in one corner, and she made her way to that one dry spot and lowered her body slowly to sit on the rock-strewn ground.

Incredibly she was shivering with cold now. This was one of those sudden rainstorms that she had heard about. They came up with little warning in this part of the world, and they disappeared as quickly. She smoothed her dripping hair away from her face, stripping water from the long strands with her fingernails as best she could. Then she pulled her knees up to her chest and hugged her legs, trying to ignore the ache in her swollen ankle, and settled herself to wait until the rain passed.

In an effort to take her mind off her predicament, she studied the crumbling remains of the building where she had found shelter. It appeared to have been small with four square pillars in front; in all likelihood it had been a place of worship to the Mayan gods.

Nevertheless, the wretchedness of her situation could not long be kept at bay. What was she doing, injured and soaked to the skin, sitting huddled beneath a pile of rubble in this godforsaken place? And what had happened to the stallion? What if he didn't return to the hacienda? What if he injured himself? What if—

Soon angry tears were tracing their way down her already wet face. If Shane hadn't ordered her to stay off the stallion, she would never have taken him out in the first place! But why stop there? If she hadn't been such a brainless idiot, she would have quit her job weeks ago and she wouldn't be in her present miserable predicament. She shivered, hugged her knees tighter, and stared out at the rain in utter desolation.

It was only after peering from her pathetic shelter for some time that she realized something was moving toward her in the rain-drenched landscape. A big, swaying apparition in yellow. It was almost upon her before she recognized Shane wearing knee-high rubber boots and a waterproof hooded poncho that fell to meet the boot tops.

He trudged to her shelter, bent, and, shaking water off the poncho, threw back the hood. "What do you think you're doing?"

She glared up and her blue-violet eyes snapped back. "Oh, just out enjoying myself! What does it look like I'm doing?"

He looked down at her, shaking his head, his yellow bulk filling the small structure. "When the stallion came back to the house saddled and riderless, I thought—"

"Is he all right?"

"*He* is fine. But I've imagined every kind of horror that could possibly befall you on the walk here!"

"Well, I'm sorry to disappoint you," she retorted, shivering harder, "but I've only sprained my ankle. I'm sure it will be good as new in a day or two. How did you know where to find me?"

"A process of elimination. Dammit, Leigh, I told you to stay off that horse!"

She stared into his cynical gray eyes, her breath drawn in with difficulty. "All right, so I should have listened. It was a stupid thing to do and I was wrong. You were right. Is that what you want to hear? You're always right!"

He stood there, his mouth a relentless line. "You're going to have pneumonia if you don't get out of those wet clothes." He shrugged off the poncho, letting it slide to the ground, and unbuttoned the long-sleeved cotton shirt he wore. "Take off that halter and put this on."

She looked mutinously at the extended shirt for a moment. "Not unless you turn your back."

She saw a flicker of a smile cross his lips before he dropped the shirt and turned away from her. She managed, in spite of violently shaking fingers, to get out of the halter and into the shirt, buttoning it to the collar. Some of his warmth remained in the cloth and it felt lovely against her cold skin. "You can turn around now," she muttered.

He had opened the front of the poncho and now sat down beside her, drawing her against his naked, warm chest and draping the poncho over both of them. "We'll stay here until the rain stops."

She huddled against him, grateful for the enveloping male warmth, her head cradled against his shoulder. "You see," he said in a low, husky voice, "I do have my uses. Do you think we might pretend, just for a little while, that we've just met."

"Oh, Shane," she whispered, "it's too late for that. I—I can't take any more."

He was silent for a while. Then, "I had a long lecture from Ben last night about the futility of false pride. I've been wanting to talk to you ever since, waiting for the right moment." He drew a long breath. "Maybe this is it. You said a while ago that I'm always right—meaning, of course, that I think I am. But you're mistaken. I've been wrong about almost everything where you are concerned. In fact, I don't seem to have been able to do anything that was *right*. Whatever I said or did seemed to hurt you or anger you, and that was never my intention. But I just kept blundering ahead, making an ass of myself. Do you know that this very morning, I had the audacity to go into San Miguel and talk to a city official?"

"What about?"

The hand that had been moving caressingly along her

upper arm under the poncho stopped and his head moved and she knew he was looking down at her. She met his gaze and saw the hardness of his gray eyes altering, melting into warmth. Then both his arms came around her swiftly, lifting her onto the warmth of his lap, as he found her mouth in a kiss that sent molten desire surging to her every sense. She clung to him, not caring that this could be her final humiliation, that he might send her away from him within days.

"Oh, Shane, if only——" she said pleadingly when he let her draw breath for a moment. Her voice was muffled against his neck.

"I want you, my darling." He turned her face to his with warm, strong fingers. "No, don't get that hurt look in your eyes. Wanting each other's bodies is a part of love between a man and a woman."

Love. . . . He had said love, she thought dazedly. And he had called her darling. He pushed the wet hair away from her face and began to kiss her forehead, her closed eyelids, her cheeks. . . . "I've been an utter fool. I fell in love with you that first night when I walked into the dining room at the ranch and saw you standing there, so young and small and beautiful—and so defiant. Oh, I didn't admit it to myself then and not for a long time afterward. I convinced myself if I could just take you to bed the feeling would pass. I've never been in love before, you know—not like this."

The eyes that looked into his were flooded with wondering adoration. "Shane, I wish——"

"Don't." He silenced her with a gentle kiss. "Let's don't waste any more time on regrets. The reason I don't want you to continue as my veterinarian is that I hope— Well, the man I talked to this morning is the official who marries people. It is very easy to get married in Mexico, my love. We could do it tomorrow, if you will only agree." His arm tightened around her. "And you had better. I am prepared to kidnap you and carry you off someplace where we'll never be found if you don't. You will marry me tomorrow, won't you?"

"Yes. Oh, yes!" She lifted her mouth to his, hands behind the dark head, holding him close. "I love you," she whispered against his lips, "and I want you. Make love to me, Shane."

His arms were gentle now, gathering her up, his mouth passionate on hers as he lifted and carried her from the shelter into the Cozumel desolation outside, where the rain had stopped. He lifted his head to look down into her face. "I intend to, my darling. But not on the hard, damp ground. I'm no shining knight, but I want everything to be right for you when we come together the first time. I have reserved a suite in Ben's hotel for tomorrow night." A devilish smile played at the corners of his mouth. "There. I told you I was audacious, didn't I? You might have said no, and then what would I have done with that luxurious suite? After a few days there, I thought we would continue our honeymoon in New Mexico."

"Where, incidentally, we will be able to take in the All American," she said teasingly.

"You don't mind, do you?"

Leigh smiled softly. "Would you change your plans if I did?"

"Well, I—" He stopped as he recognized the teasing twinkle in her eyes. Then he said with a wicked look, "Certainly not. A wife must learn to follow where her husband leads."

"We may," she murmured contentedly, "have to pursue that subject at a later time."

He laughed heartily. "Oh, my love, I am sure of it."

She snuggled against him, secure in the strength of his arms, as he carried her toward the hacienda. In that moment Leigh gave herself willingly into his hands. Their marriage would not always run smoothly. They were both too strong-willed for that. But she knew she would love this big, arrogant, domineering man for the rest of her life.

Love—the way you want it!

Candlelight Romances

		TITLE NO.	
☐ A MAN OF HER CHOOSING by Nina Pykare $1.50		#554	(15133-3)
☐ PASSING FANCY by Mary Linn Roby $1.50		#555	(16770-1)
☐ THE DEMON COUNT by Anne Stuart $1.25		#557	(11906-5)
☐ WHERE SHADOWS LINGER by Janis Susan May $1.25		#556	(19777-5)
☐ OMEN FOR LOVE by Esther Boyd $1.25		#552	(16108-8)
☐ MAYBE TOMORROW by Marie Pershing $1.25		#553	(14909-6)
☐ LOVE IN DISGUISE by Nina Pykare $1.50		#548	(15229-1)
☐ THE RUNAWAY HEIRESS by Lillian Cheatham $1.50		#549	(18083-X)
☐ HOME TO THE HIGHLANDS by Jessica Eliot $1.25		#550	(13104-9)
☐ DARK LEGACY by Candace Connell $1.25		#551	(11771-2)
☐ LEGACY OF THE HEART by Lorena McCourtney $1.25		#546	(15645-9)
☐ THE SLEEPING HEIRESS by Phyllis Taylor Pianka $1.50		#543	(17551-8)
☐ DAISY by Jennie Tremaine $1.50		#542	(11683-X)
☐ RING THE BELL SOFTLY by Margaret James $1.25		#545	(17626-3)
☐ GUARDIAN OF INNOCENCE by Judy Boynton $1.25		#544	(11862-X)
☐ THE LONG ENCHANTMENT by Helen Nuelle $1.25		#540	(15407-3)
☐ SECRET LONGINGS by Nancy Kennedy $1.25		#541	(17609-3)

At your local bookstore or use this handy coupon for ordering:

DELL BOOKS
P.O. BOX 1000, PINEBROOK, N.J. 07058

Please send me the books I have checked above. I am enclosing $_____
(please add 75¢ per copy to cover postage and handling). Send check or money
order—no cash or C.O.D.'s. Please allow up to 8 weeks for shipment.

Mr/Mrs/Miss _____

Address _____

City _____ State/Zip _____

THE DARK HORSEMAN

Marianne Harvey

author of *The Proud Hunter*

Beautiful Donna Penroze had sworn to her dying father that she would save her sole legacy, the crumbling tin mines and the ancient, desolate estate *Trencobban*. But the mines were failing, and Donna had no one to turn to. No one except the mysterious Nicholas Trevarvas—rich, arrogant, commanding. Donna would do anything but surrender her pride, anything but admit her irresistible longing for *The Dark Horseman*.

A Dell Book $3.25

The passionate sequel to
the scorching novel of
fierce pride and forbidden love

THE PROUD HUNTER

by Marianne Harvey

Author of *The Dark Horseman* and *The Wild One*

Trefyn Connor—he demanded all that was his—and more—with the arrogance of a man who fought to win . . . with the passion of a man who meant to possess his enemy's daughter and make her pay the price!

Juliet Trevarvas—the beautiful daughter of The Dark Horseman. She would make Trefyn come to her. She would taunt him, shock him, claim him body and soul before she would surrender to THE PROUD HUNTER.

A Dell Book $3.25   (17098-2)